The
Lost
Track
of
Time

The
Lost

Track of Time

BY Paige Britt

DRAWINGS BY LEE WHITE

SCHOLASTIC PRESS

NEW YORK

LIBRARY OF CONGRESS CATALOGING-IN-PUBLICATION DATA

Britt, Paige, author.
The lost track of time / by Paige Britt; drawings by Lee White.
— First edition.   pages   cm
Summary: Penelope is an imaginative girl, whose every day has been rigidly scheduled
by her mother—until one day she falls through a hole in her calendar and lands in the
Realm of Possibility, where she discovers that it, too, is stuck in a track of time, and
only she can save it.
  1. Time—Juvenile fiction. 2. Imagination—Juvenile fiction.
  3. Self-actualization (Psychology)—Juvenile fiction.
  4. Mothers and daughters—Juvenile fiction.
  [1. Time—Fiction. 2. Imagination—Fiction.
  3. Self-actualization (Psychology)—Fiction.
  4. Mothers and daughters—Fiction.]
  I. White, Lee, 1970− illustrator. II. Title.
  PZ7.B78065Los 2015   [Fic]—dc23   2014012529

ISBN 978-0-545-53812-1
10 9 8 7 6 5 4 3 2 1   15 16 17 18 19

Printed in Singapore   46
First edition, April 2015

chapter one

Beep. Beep. Beep. Beep.

Penelope dragged one eye open and then the other. She'd been dreaming about a fire-eating lizard that spoke in riddles. The lizard was right in the middle of telling her something important when the alarm went off. She glared at the clock. It glared back: 6:00 a.m.

Here it was, the first day of summer vacation, and even now her mother expected her to get up and get busy. Penelope shut off the beeping and sat up. She dangled her feet over the bed and stared down at her toes. She had to be showered, dressed, and ready for breakfast in 30 minutes, which meant she'd better hurry. She wondered what it would be like to have a day off. Just once.

This won't take long, she told herself. Penelope dropped to the floor and began rummaging underneath her bed for one of the notebooks she kept hidden there.

Penelope's room was extremely neat. Her mother was fond of saying, "A place for everything and everything in its place." That's why Penelope kept everything that had no place in her room underneath the bed. There was the hamster habitat she was building (Penelope didn't own a hamster), the diary she was writing for her twin sister lost at sea (Penelope was an only child), and the invisible ink kit for sending secret messages (just in case she ever got stuck in a Turkish prison). And of course, there were the notebooks. Piles of

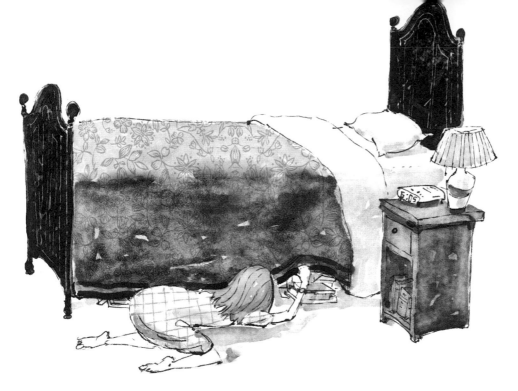

notebooks filled with all the fascinating words she had collected over the years and all the stories she had written with them.

Penelope pushed aside a box of hamster food and pulled out a small red notebook. She flipped it open and used the pencil tucked between its pages to make a quick sketch of the lizard from her dream — big eyes, long body, and a curling tongue, licking up bits of flame. When she finished, she sat back and tried to think of a name for the creature. It wasn't like naming a dog or a cat. It had to be unusual, like Beauregard or Eckbert. No. Too complicated. She needed something simple like . . . Zak. That was it!

Now that she had a name, what next? Zak couldn't just eat fire and speak in riddles. He needed an adventure. Penelope chewed on her pencil to help her think.

The smell of bacon drifted up from the kitchen and her stomach growled. She chewed harder. Maybe Zak belonged to a circus made up entirely of reptiles . . . or maybe he lived in a volcano that was about to blow up the world . . . or . . .

Bacon!

Penelope dropped her pencil. She realized what the smell meant. She was late. Her mother had started making breakfast, and Penelope was expected at the table. She shoved her notebook back under the bed, tore off her pajamas, and threw on some clothes. She raced down the stairs, combing her hair with her fingers. As soon as she stepped into the kitchen, her mother gave her "the look."

"Do you *know* what time it is?"

Penelope slid into her chair. "I know," she mumbled. Penelope couldn't tell the truth — that she'd lost track of time. Her mother wouldn't understand. Not when there was a clock in every room of the house and a watch on her wrist. Just because Penelope wore a watch, though, didn't mean she looked at it. It made her nervous. The second hand never sat still. It swung around and around, sweeping the day away like sand.

Penelope's mother put breakfast on the table and sat down. "Your father will be back from his run any minute now, so we'd better get started." She reached across the table for her leather three-ring binder. "Let's see what's on the schedule for today, shall we?"

Here we go, thought Penelope, slumping over her plate.

"Sit up straight," said her mother without looking up.

Penelope felt a knot form in her stomach as she waited for her mother to begin. The binder held a calendar that served as Penelope's schedule. Each page was a single day and each day was filled with a long list of things she was expected to do. Penelope's mother ripped yesterday's page off the calendar and let out a satisfied sigh. "Looks like you've got a full day ahead of you." She held out the calendar for Penelope to see.

There was the month (May), the date (29), and the quote from Poor Richard (whoever *he* was). After that, lines and lines of her mother's neat handwriting filled the page:

May 29

Be always ashamed to catch thyself idle.

6:30–7:00 Breakfast

7:00–7:30 Daily chores

7:30–8:30 Piano practice

8:30–8:45 Free time

8:45–9:15 Drive to dentist

9:15–10:15 Dentist appt.

10:15–10:45 Drive home from dentist

10:45–11:45 SAT vocabulary drills

11:45–12:15 Wash and polish bike

12:15–12:30 Ride bike

12:30–1:00 Lunch

1:00–2:00 Math tutoring

2:00–3:00 Write b-day thank-you cards NEATLY!

3:00–4:30 Get started on summer reading list

4:30–5:30 Cooking lesson

5:30–6:30 Dinner

6:30–6:45 Free time

6:45–7:00 Call Grandma

7:00–8:00 Tidy room and get ready for bed

Penelope's mother cleared her throat and began to read off all the day's activities. As she did, Penelope wondered for the hundredth time just *who* Poor Richard was. Even though she had never met him, she didn't like him. He was always saying things about "industry" or "sloth." What exactly was *sloth*? It seemed like it had something to do with being lazy. But then again, wasn't a sloth an animal that looked like a sock puppet? Maybe a sloth would make a good sidekick for Zak, the fire-eating lizard . . .

"Penelope!"

Penelope looked up. Her mother was staring at her expectantly. "I *said*, hurry and finish your breakfast. It's almost time for your daily chores."

Just then, the front door swung open and a voice called out, "I'm home!" A minute later her father bounded into the kitchen.

"Hi, pumpkin," he said and rumpled Penelope's hair. "It's another beautiful day out there." He pronounced the word *beautiful* as if it were three words — *beau-ti-ful*.

"How did it go, dear?" asked her mother, flipping to the back of the binder where she kept an account of his daily runs — time, date, distance.

"Great! Five miles, 41:4."

Penelope's mother recorded the information and shut the binder. "Your day is off to a good start," she said, as if the numbers proved it.

"It certainly is!" Her father downed a glass of water and then sat at the table to peel a banana. "I bet you have a lot to look forward to today, huh, kiddo?" he said and reached for the paper.

Penelope crammed a piece of toast in her mouth and mumbled something unintelligible. Her dad wouldn't understand. He looked forward to *every* day. He was an insurance agent, and although he helped people prepare for disasters — death, disease, fire — he was so happy all the time you would have thought he worked at Disneyland.

Penelope finished her toast and got up from the table.

"I guess I'd better get started on my chores."

Her dad glanced up from the sports page. "Go get 'em, tiger," he said, giving her a thumbs-up.

Her mother, who was on the phone, just waved.

Monday was Penelope's day to vacuum the living and dining room floors. As she walked back and forth, vacuuming in neat lines, she thought about the other kids in her class. They probably had summers filled with nothing but hanging out at the pool all day and going to slumber parties at night. Penelope had never been to a slumber party in her life. "Early to bed, early to rise," was another one of Poor Richard's rules.

Penelope changed the vacuum attachment and began sucking up the dirt and crumbs between the couch cushions. She knew it was no use complaining about her schedule. No matter how packed it was, her mother's was even worse. Penelope's mother was an event planner. She planned parties, business meetings, weddings, bar mitzvahs, and anything else that needed to go perfectly. From what Penelope could tell, her mother spent all her time on the phone or the computer organizing other people's lives. Apparently no one minded, because they gave her money to do it.

Penelope knew she should feel lucky to get her mother's help for free, but she didn't. Her mother said that following a daily schedule was the best way to prepare for the future. Penelope didn't know how she could prepare for something that was so impossible to imagine. She could hardly picture herself graduating from middle school, much less going to college. Besides, the only thing she wanted to do was be a writer. Last year her English teacher,

Mr. Gomez, had given her a magazine full of stories written by kids her age. "Keep reading and keep writing," he had told her. "And when you're ready, you should send this magazine one of your stories. I think you have a real chance of getting published." She couldn't get his words out of her mind.

Penelope finished vacuuming the living room and moved on to the dining room. The only other person who encouraged Penelope to write was her neighbor, Miss Maddie. When Penelope was little, before she started school, her mother would drop her off at Miss Maddie's house whenever she had a business meeting to attend or an errand to run. Once in a while, Penelope spent the whole day at Miss Maddie's house. Even though it was just down the street, it felt like a different world. At Miss Maddie's house, Penelope was allowed to do what her mother would call "nothing." It wasn't the nothing where you watched TV for hours, waiting for the day to pass. This nothing was more like a blank page Penelope could fill however she wanted.

Whenever Penelope stayed with Miss Maddie, she would spend all her time reading, writing, or just staring out the window. Miss Maddie didn't mind; in fact, she often joined in. Once they had spent an entire afternoon looking for faces in the wood grain of Miss Maddie's dining room table. After they found a face, they drew it on a piece of paper and gave it a name like "Ichabod" or "Millicent." Next they made up elaborate stories about the characters, which

Penelope wrote down in a notebook. Whenever Penelope asked if they were wasting time, Miss Maddie would just roll her eyes and say, "Don't you worry about the time, it'll keep track of itself."

Penelope wished she believed that.

The grandfather clock chimed 7:30 a.m. and Penelope turned off the vacuum cleaner. "Time for piano practice!" her mother called from the other room.

"I know, I know!" Penelope called back.

She put away the machine as fast as she could and ran down the hall to the living room. She had exactly one hour to complete her sight-reading and theory exercises, practice her scales, and play through all the music assigned by her piano teacher. If she finished by 8:30, she could use her free time to visit with Miss Maddie.

Penelope rushed through her scales and then played all her practice pieces. The piano theory and sight-reading worksheets took longer to complete, and by the time she finished, her hour was almost up. She slammed her workbook closed and headed for the back door. "I'm going to Miss Maddie's," she called over her shoulder.

"Be back in fifteen minutes!" her mother shouted after her. "We leave for the dentist at 8:45 sharp!"

Penelope could almost feel the seconds ticking away as she ran down the street toward Miss Maddie's house. Miss Maddie had lived at the end of Ginger Lane even before there *was* a Ginger Lane or any such thing as the Spicewood Estates housing development. She had once shown Penelope a faded black-and-white picture of her house surrounded by a wide-open field and tall oak trees. Instead of Ginger Lane, a long dirt road ran up to the front gate.

"Once they sold this land and began building Spicewood Estates, houses sprouted up overnight," Miss Maddie had said.

As she ran, Penelope imagined she was racing through a field with houses popping up out of the ground, each with a door, two windows, and a driveway.

Miss Maddie's house wasn't like anyone else's house. It didn't have a mailbox perched on the corner of a neat lawn and a walkway dotted with flowers. Instead, it had an old paint-chipped fence covered with ivy. The front yard had a patch of sunflowers, an overgrown herb garden, and an enormous oak tree. The oak tree spread out across the yard, with branches that almost touched the ground. A pathway ran through the front gate, around the tree, and stopped at a bright purple door.

No one in all of Spicewood Estates had a purple door.

No one except Miss Maddie.

Penelope opened the gate and hurried up the path. She would have preferred to take her time. Sometimes she found stray items along the way — glossy wrappers, colored string, or small toys. Miss Maddie told her that birds would often spot shiny objects on the ground and use them in their nests. Penelope suspected that the little treasures she found were gifts from Miss Maddie meant for the birds.

Today, however, Penelope didn't have time to scavenge for shiny objects. She rushed up to the door and used their secret knock.

Knock-knock-knock. Knock. Knock.

Miss Maddie flung open the door. "What a nice surprise!"

"I've only . . . got . . . a minute," said Penelope, trying to catch her breath.

"Nonsense," said Miss Maddie. "You've got all the time in the world."

Miss Maddie was always saying things like that. Things that made no sense. As far as Penelope was concerned, time was like a bank account, and she was overdrawn.

"I *don't* have all the time in the world," insisted Penelope. "You haven't seen my schedule today."

"Nor do I want to." Miss Maddie stepped back to let Penelope in. "Don't suppose you have time for tea?"

Penelope shook her head.

"All right then, let's just have a sit."

At Miss Maddie's house "a sit" was a very special thing. But then again, it wasn't. It was a little bit like waiting, but at the same time, not like waiting at all. Penelope couldn't quite figure it out. It involved sitting down in a chair and doing nothing. It was wonderful.

Penelope followed Miss Maddie into the living room. A thick rug covered the floor like grass. Miss Maddie had told her it was a Persian rug. *Persian*. It was one of the first words Penelope had ever collected in her notebook. Just the sound of it gave her a shiver of pleasure.

A deep fireplace that burnt real logs took up one end of the room. At the other end, a bay window looked out on Miss Maddie's unruly front yard. There were no curtains on the window. Instead, the sprawling oak tree blocked the view of the street.

As beautiful and exotic as these things were, the best thing about the room was its silence. Not one clock ticked, tocked, chimed, or donged. There wasn't a clock on the mantle or on the wall or on the coffee table. In fact, Penelope had never seen a clock *anywhere* in Miss Maddie's house.

When Penelope had asked her about the missing clocks, Miss Maddie had just shrugged. "I don't need clocks to tell me what time it is. I always do things at the same exact time anyway."

"Really?" Penelope had said. "At the same *exact* time?"

"Yes, ma'am. I do things in my own sweet time. *Every* time."

Penelope couldn't imagine what it must be like not to have a schedule to follow. Having "a sit" with Miss Maddie was the closest she ever got to her "own sweet time." She settled herself in a comfy chair in front of the bay window and curled up her legs. Miss Maddie sat next to her, hands resting loosely on her lap. A hush settled over the room and the sitting began.

Penelope stared at the sunlight playing with the leaves on the oak tree. After a while, a hush crept into her mind and the sunlight stopped being sunlight and the leaves stopped being leaves and for the briefest, smallest moment everything was everything until . . .

Ring!

Penelope sat bolt upright. She glanced over at Miss Maddie. Miss Maddie was still staring out the window, hands in her lap.

Ring!

"The phone is ringing," Penelope blurted out.

"Yup," said Miss Maddie with a slight nod. "That's what they do."

Ring!

It occurred to Penelope that it might be her mother.

"Aren't you going to get it?"

Miss Maddie sighed and got up from her chair.

Penelope wondered how long she had been sitting there. It only felt like a minute, but it could have been longer. There really was only one way to find out. Slowly, slowly Penelope looked down at her wristwatch. For a second, the numbers were nothing but little black marks marching around in a circle. Then they came into focus and Penelope read the time:

8:46.

She was late.

chapter two

At dinner that evening, her mother made an announcement. "Penelope, your father and I have discussed it, and we think it best that you no longer visit Miss Maddie."

Penelope stared at her, fork frozen in midair.

"I know Miss Maddie meant a lot to you when you were little, and heaven knows I appreciated her help looking after you, but now that you're older, I think you need to focus on the future. I've already called and told her not to expect you any longer. So it's settled." She took a large bite of her steak and began to chew.

Penelope looked at her dad. He just shrugged. "Your mother is in charge of your schedule, pal. Besides, she has so many great things planned for you this summer, you're not going to want to miss any of them. Just think, science camp starts in a few days."

Penelope could feel dinner turning to stone in her stomach. She swallowed hard. "But *why*?" she finally blurted out.

"We don't think it's the best use of your time," her mother answered.

"I hardly have any free time as it is," pleaded Penelope.

Penelope's mother placed her fork neatly on her plate and fixed Penelope with a stare. "Time isn't free, Penelope. And neither is college. Do you know how much an Ivy League school costs?"

Penelope shook her head. She didn't even know what an Ivy League school was.

"I can tell you, it costs a lot. How do you expect us to pay for college if you don't get a scholarship? If you weren't so caught up in your fantasies, you would be farther along in your studies. You would be more productive. More *competitive*."

Penelope sat very still, struggling to focus on what her mother had just said. *If she wasn't so caught up in her fantasies, she would be more competitive?* What was she competing for? Why did her mother treat life like it was a race against time? No matter what Penelope did, she always fell behind.

"Speaking of scholarships," continued her mother, "you'll be taking the pre-pre-SAT this year and you need to be ready. From now on, I want you to focus your writing on the sample essay questions I give you. No more scribbling in your notebook."

Penelope gasped. *Scribbling?* She wasn't scribbling — she was *writing*. There was a difference.

"Hey there, buddy," said her dad. "Your mom is only trying to do what's best for you."

Penelope exhaled slowly. "They're not scribbles," she finally said, trying to keep her voice steady.

"What?" asked her mother, who was busy cutting her steak.

"My notebook. They aren't scribbles. They're stories. Mr. Gomez said I could even be published one day —"

"Stories don't pay the bills, Penelope," said her mother, cutting her off. "In today's economy we can't afford to be impractical."

"Pass the potatoes, will you, sport?" said her father.

Penelope opened her mouth, then closed it. It was no use arguing. Her parents didn't listen anyway. Now there was to be no more writing in her notebook. No more visits to Miss Maddie. No more nothing. "May I be excused?" she asked, pushing back from the table.

"Not yet," said her mother. "I knew you'd be disappointed about not getting to visit Miss Maddie, so I bought you a little something to cheer you up." She put down her fork and napkin and got up from the table. "I'll be right back."

She returned a moment later with a package. Inside the package was a book. The cover featured a man wearing a suit, looking extremely pleased with himself. He was holding up a long to-do list. Next to each entry was a bright red check mark.

"It's your very own copy of *Getting Everything Done*," said her mother excitedly. "I have one, too. I just couldn't *live* without it."

Penelope flipped through the book, trying to think of something nice to say. She stopped when she came to an illustration featuring a series of squares with tiny arrows running back and forth between them. The man stood to the side, pointing at the illustration with a ruler.

"That's a work-flow diagram," explained her mother. "You won't believe how helpful it is. Each square represents a task you need to do and the arrows tell you when to do it. It will make you so much more organized. You're just going to love it!" She beamed down at Penelope. "I'll clear your calendar for the evening. You go ahead and read your book."

Penelope bolted from the table, ran upstairs, and threw the book face-down on her desk. There was the man again! He was posed for a portrait on the back cover, arms crossed, a smug smile on his face. He was wearing a gray suit, gray shirt, and gray tie. Everything about him was the same dull color, except for his teeth, which were unnaturally white. Below the picture was a "personal message." Penelope read:

My work on human productivity resource allocation is the latest and, if I may say so, greatest of the century! If you utilize my proven methods, you'll be a success like me. You'll get everything done! In this book I'll tell you how to follow my time-saving tips and monitor your hourly progress. I'll tell you exactly how to overhaul the logistics of daily life, break down the elements of your must-do tasks, and actualize the hidden potential in the micromoments between project steps.

Ugh. How boring, thought Penelope. She shoved the book in her desk drawer and plopped down on the bed. How on earth could she get through to her parents? Words weren't enough. That was obvious. Her father only listened to her mother and her mother only listened to proof. But how could Penelope *prove* her stories were important? *If I don't do something, my whole life will turn into a work-flow diagram!*

Penelope heard the *thump-thump-thump* of someone running up the stairs. A moment later there was a quick rap on the door and her dad poked his head in. "Hey, pal! Got a minute?"

Penelope shrugged. "I guess so."

"Great!" Her father stepped inside and grabbed the desk chair, flipping it around to face Penelope. He sat down and leaned forward, propping his elbows on his knees. "Time for a pep talk," he announced.

Not again, thought Penelope. Pep talks were her dad's favorite form of communication.

"You know," he said, launching into his speech, "I meant what I said at the dinner table. Your mom really does want what's best for you. All this planning and organizing, it's for your own good."

"I *do* know," said Penelope, who had heard this all before. "But why is it that what I want isn't good enough? She never lets me do my own thing. She only wants me to do *her* thing."

"She doesn't want you to miss out on any opportunities for success. Trust me, she knows what she's doing. I used to sell hot dogs at football games until I met your mother. Now I'm an insurance agent." He sat back in his chair. "Not bad, huh, kid?"

Penelope fought the urge to roll her eyes.

"Just wait and see. Your mom has a plan for your life. It's going to be top-notch."

"But I want to be a writer," Penelope insisted.

"Well, sport, writing is a little iffy." He wobbled his hand back and forth. "I say, life is already full of surprises. Why not go for a sure thing?" He put his fists up like a boxer and began making little jabs at the air. "You've got to be prepared. Ahead of the game. On the ball." He dropped his hands and gave Penelope a meaningful look. "Got it?"

Before Penelope could say a word, he gave her a soft punch on the arm. "'Course you do. That's my girl."

Penelope knew this meant the pep talk was over. He liked to keep them short, which was fine with her.

Sure enough, her father rose to his feet. "I'm glad we had this talk," he said. "See you in the morning?"

"Sure," said Penelope. "See you in the morning."

As soon as the door clicked shut, Penelope fell back on her bed with a groan. Her dad's pep talks always left her exhausted. The person she *really* needed to talk to was Miss Maddie, but she was off-limits. Once Miss Maddie had told her, "When faced with a challenge you have to fight fire with fire!" Penelope wondered what that meant.

Fight fire with fire.

It didn't make any sense. Fighting fire with fire would just make things worse, wouldn't it? Penelope imagined a bonfire growing out of control. You wouldn't fight it by throwing more burning logs on it. That was feeding the fire. You would fight it with water. But that's not what Miss Maddie had said. Penelope knew that fire ate everything in its path. Maybe you *couldn't* stop it. Maybe you just had to let it burn. That didn't seem right either.

Penelope closed her eyes and pretended she was sitting in Miss Maddie's living room. There was the big window and the giant oak tree and the bright blue sky and . . . A thought popped into her head: *If you fight fire with fire, maybe you aren't really trying to put it out.*

Penelope sat up.

She might be onto something. She jumped out of bed, pulled open her desk drawer, and stole another look at the book her mother had given her. There was the man, holding up his to-do list, smiling like he was king of the world.

I could make my own to-do list, she thought.

Her heart skipped a beat.

A list with tasks to accomplish my *goals . . .*

A list of things I *want to do!*

Penelope slammed the drawer shut. Maybe that was it! Maybe that's what fighting fire with fire meant. Maybe you could solve a problem by using the same stuff that made it a problem in the first place.

Penelope grabbed a piece of paper and began to write her very own to-do list. Next to each item, she placed a small box, just waiting for a check mark.

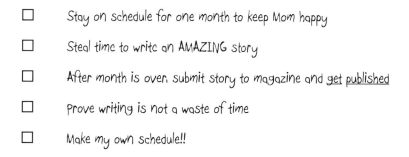

☐ Stay on schedule for one month to keep Mom happy

☐ Steal time to write an AMAZING story

☐ After month is over, submit story to magazine and get published

☐ Prove writing is not a waste of time

☐ Make my own schedule!!

From that moment on, Penelope did everything right on time. She got up at 6:00, dressed, and brushed her teeth. She reached the breakfast table at exactly 6:30 and sat up straight while her mother conducted the daily schedule review. She consulted her wristwatch throughout the day and made sure she was exactly where she needed to be, when she needed to be.

"Seems like that book was a big help," said her dad on the way to science camp a few days later. "Look how smoothly everything is going already!"

Penelope, who was staring out the window, just nodded. She was trying to think up an amazing story idea. Maybe she would write about a super-genius kid who created an endless energy source from bubble gum. Everybody chewed gum all day to power the lights in their houses.

Honk! Honk!

Penelope looked up. Her dad had pulled up to the drop-off zone at the community center where science camp was held. He was waiting for Penelope to get out and so was a line of cars behind them. "Wake up, buddy! It's time to go," he said. Penelope grabbed her backpack and jumped out. Her dad waved apologetically to the car behind him and sped off.

A counselor was waiting at the curb to give Penelope her group assignment. "You're part of the Mad Scientists this week!" she announced cheerfully. "Room 203."

Penelope thought about this for a minute. She wasn't exactly *mad*, she decided, but she wasn't very happy either. She had wanted to go to summer camp, just not for science. Mr. Gomez was teaching a creative writing workshop at the library, but her mother had said no.

"Jobs of the future are in high tech or health care sectors," her mother droned, dropping two brochures on the table. "You can go to computer camp or science camp. Take your pick."

Penelope picked science camp. At least there were experiments.

She glanced at her wristwatch and hurried down the hall to her room. A woman with short brown hair introduced herself as "Ms. Romine." She wore a lab coat and sipped coffee from a beaker.

"Hello, Mad Scientists!" Ms. Romine announced when everyone had taken their seats. "Welcome to the first day of science camp. Today's topic is mushrooms. Does anyone know the difference between a mushroom and a plant?"

Nineteen hands shot up in the air.

Penelope slid down in her chair. Apparently she was the only one at camp who didn't know anything about mushrooms. Well, she knew *one* thing. She didn't like them. They tasted musty. And slimy. And old.

"Mushrooms are a vital part of our ecosystem," continued Ms. Romine. "In fact, fungi are one of the most important organisms on the planet! You might even say they have a role to play in every part of our lives — from food production to waste management."

Penelope found this extremely hard to believe. Everyone else, though, was madly taking notes. Penelope propped her chin on her hand and stared out the window.

Just then Ms. Romine clapped her hands. "All right, everyone, partner up with the person next to you. We're going to work on mushroom identification."

The boy at the desk next to Penelope's was named Ebon. She knew him from Quiz Bowl competition.

"Did you know that some mushrooms have a body that spreads out over several miles?" Ebon asked as soon as they'd pushed their desks together.

Before Penelope could answer, the girl with pigtails seated in front of them swiveled around. "I know. They're called mycorrhizal associations."

Why are you even in science camp if you know everything already? wondered Penelope.

Ms. Romine passed out fungi identification charts, and the rest of the morning was spent drawing and labeling the parts of different mushrooms. That afternoon they took small samples from the mushrooms and looked at them under a microscope. While Ebon recorded the cell diameter of the various samples, Penelope thought about story ideas. Her story needed to be something her parents would like. Maybe a story about a girl who got a perfect score on the SATs and graduated from college at sixteen and became president of the United States. Or maybe a story about a boy who had an internal clock that told him what time it was no matter where in the world he was. He had super-turbo-charged feet and could run faster than the speed of light so he was never late.

Nah. Neither of those seemed right.

When camp was over for the day, Penelope couldn't wait to get home and see if she could come up with something better. She ate dinner as fast as she could. By the time she finished picking up her room and getting ready for bed, she was too tired to concentrate, but she dug her red notebook out from under the bed anyway. A few ideas came to mind.

A girl who starts a business and makes a million dollars . . .

A boy who is smarter than a computer . . .

A really organized kid who can speed-read . . .

Ugh. These were horrible!

"Lights out!" called her mother from downstairs.

Already? Penelope reluctantly turned out the lights and slipped her notebook under the bed. *I'll come up with something better tomorrow,* she told herself.

Penelope rolled over on her back and closed her eyes, letting her mind wander to one of its favorite places . . . After she finished her story, her mother would love it so much that she would clear Penelope's schedule. Every day would be wide open. Filled with nothing. Penelope's stories would be so good her mother would let her display her notebooks on the bookshelf in her bedroom. No more digging them out from underneath the bed. Maybe someday someone would buy what she'd written and there would be a whole shelf in the library filled with her stories. She would be a famous author and travel the world looking for inspiration. She'd travel by hot air balloon, so she could see all the sights. Birds would land on the balloon's basket and she'd tie little notes to their feet, just like messages in a bottle . . .

Penelope drifted off to sleep, where her fantasies took flight and turned into dreams.

chapter three

The next day was very much like the one before except for one thing: homework. Ms. Romine didn't call it that. She called it a "science project," but Penelope knew better.

"This is the perfect thing for a work-flow diagram!" exclaimed her mother when she heard of the assignment. "We'll make one together right after dinner."

Penelope cringed. How was she going to steal time to write if her mother kept crowding her schedule?

As soon as the table was cleared, her mother got busy breaking down the project into tasks and something called "deliverables." Penelope had never heard of a deliverable before, but she had a pretty good idea what it meant. A deliverable must be something you delivered or turned in. Proof that you did something.

Penelope thought about her checklist. *Just wait. In a month, I'm going to turn in my* own *deliverable — the most amazing story ever!*

After identifying the project deliverables, her mother created a timeline. Penelope was shocked to see the entire week mapped out in tiny segments. It looked like her daily schedule, but blown up and stretched out. Was this the future? The future Penelope couldn't imagine? Instead of being wide open and full of possibilities, it was a series of little boxes.

For the rest of the week, each night after dinner was devoted to the science project. All Penelope wanted to do was go to her room and write, but she told herself that keeping her mother happy would pay off in the long run. The only problem was that as soon as she finished one task, another one seemed to pop up. Penelope started carrying her small red notebook in her back pocket and used any spare time during science camp to write down story ideas, but none of them seemed good enough.

It was odd. Ever since she started keeping better track of time, the less of it there seemed to be. The better she got at following her schedule, the busier it became. She was constantly checking the clock to make sure she didn't fall behind, but she fell behind anyway.

On the last night of science camp, Penelope had to work through dinner and late into the night to finish her project. She crawled under the covers, exhausted from the day and ready for sleep, but when she closed her eyes sleep wouldn't come. She tossed this way and that, her head full of worries about getting everything done.

A month has passed, and I still haven't written my story.

Once I finish science camp, Mom expects me to work on those essay questions.

Penelope flipped over onto her side.

If I don't ace those essay questions, I'll never get a scholarship.

Maybe I won't even make it into college.

But if I don't finish this story, I'll never be a writer . . .

She flipped over onto her other side.

Even if I were a writer, who would buy my stories anyway?

I'd probably end up homeless, eating tuna out of a can!

Somehow she managed to fall into a dreamless sleep only to wake the next morning and start all over. It was the last day of camp and Penelope's project won an honorable mention. Her mother was delighted, but Penelope was too tired to care. She moved through the next day and the days that followed on autopilot. By the time another week had passed, she was no closer to coming up with a story idea than before. Science camp was over, but Penelope's schedule was busier than ever. Now she was taking tennis lessons, learning Mandarin, and doing volunteer service hours at the museum in the afternoon.

One morning, Penelope forced herself to wake up before the alarm. She dug out her notebook from under the bed and opened it. She stared at the page, willing herself to write, but for the first time ever nothing came. Not even bad ideas. Her mind was blank. Not blank as in wide open, waiting for something wonderful, but blank like a wall.

That's odd, thought Penelope. She usually had more ideas than she could keep track of. She got out a few old notebooks from under her bed and flipped through them. Detailed notes, elaborate doodles, long lists of words she'd collected, and half-written stories filled the pages. None of them looked familiar. She didn't even remember writing them.

By now she should be writing madly, dreaming up new characters and creating exciting plot twists. But she wasn't. She *couldn't*. Penelope heard her mother's heels clicking down the hall. She threw on her overalls, stuffed a pen and her red notebook in her back pocket, and ran downstairs to breakfast.

"Good morning, sunshine," her mother chirped. "What'll it be?"

"Just some cereal," said Penelope. She wasn't feeling hungry. She wasn't feeling *anything*.

Once breakfast was laid out neatly, her mother sat down. "All right then, let's see what we have to look forward to today." She picked up the calendar and ripped off yesterday's date.

Penelope braced herself for the little sigh her mother always made at this point. But she didn't sigh. Instead, she let out a gasp.

Penelope put down her spoon. "What?"

"Nothing," said her mom and sat back stunned.

"Nothing?"

Penelope's mother nodded slowly.

"Nothing *what*?" Penelope prodded.

"*Nothing*, nothing. That's just it. There's absolutely nothing on the calendar today."

Penelope craned her neck to get a better look. There was the month (July), the date (3), and the quote, but after that the calendar was empty:

July 3

One today is worth two tomorrows.

Penelope's mother frowned at the blank page. "Why is there a hole in your schedule? I'm certain I had you booked until school started." She flipped through the calendar. Sure enough, all the pages were crammed with tiny black notations. When she flipped back to the blank page, she noticed a tiny smudge on the corner. "The pages must have stuck together and now you have nothing to do today," she complained, rubbing at the smudge with her thumb.

This was what Penelope had been dreaming of — an entire day of nothing! Her mind started to race. Maybe her mother would give her the day off. After all, Penelope had been on time all day, every day, for weeks and weeks. A day off wouldn't hurt. She would sit at her desk, stare out the window, and . . .

"All right," said Penelope's mother, "we'd better get busy."

Penelope's mind came to a screeching halt. "Busy? Doing what?"

"What do you mean, 'doing what?' You can't do *nothing* all day."

A familiar knot of dread formed in Penelope's stomach.

"Let's see," said her mother. "We'll start the day with another cooking lesson — you still haven't learned how to make Chicken *Cordon Bleu* — followed by ironing and Mandarin vocabulary drills. This afternoon I'd like you to replant your tomato patch. Your rows are crooked. After dinner, I think you should take up knitting. How does that sound?" She looked at Penelope expectantly, one pencil-thin eyebrow raised as high as it would go.

The knot in Penelope's stomach grew tighter.

"Penelope? I *said*, how does that sound?"

The knot moved from her stomach and into her throat. Penelope took a deep breath. "Can I have a day off instead?" she asked, pushing the words out as best she could.

"Certainly not!" her mother laughed.

"But I've been on time for weeks and weeks . . ."

"Penelope, we've been through this before. There's not the least possibility you can have a day off and get everything done. Now then, help me figure out what to do with the time slot after lunch."

Penelope stared as her mother reached for a pen.

"I know what — you can clean out all the junk under your bed. I've been wanting to do that for weeks."

"What junk?" Penelope's voice was barely a whisper.

Penelope's mother gave her an exasperated look. "You *know* what junk. Those broken toys, that useless hamster cage, not to mention those ratty old notebooks. The new school year begins soon. It's time for a fresh start, don't you think?"

Penelope wanted to yell, "NO!" But the knot in her throat wouldn't let her. Those weren't ratty old notebooks. They were her stories. She'd been a fool to think she could fight fire with fire, and now her plan had gone up in smoke. Penelope watched, unable to move or speak as her mother began to write.

But just at that moment — the *exact* moment when pen touched paper — the doorbell rang.

Ding-dong.

"Oh, dear," said her mother. "Your father must have forgotten his key." She got up from the table and walked briskly toward the front door.

As soon as her mother left the room, Penelope let out the breath she was holding and her head began to clear. There was only one person who could help save her notebooks — help save her dreams! Penelope had just a few seconds to act. It was now or never. She leaned forward, ripped the page out of the calendar, and stuffed it into her pocket. Then she slipped off her wristwatch and shoved it in a drawer before bolting out the back door.

"How'd *you* get here?" said Miss Maddie when she found Penelope at her doorstep.

"There's a hole in my schedule," said Penelope, panting.

"How extraordinary." Miss Maddie motioned Penelope inside, then closed the door. "Does your mother know you're here?"

Penelope shook her head. "No, but I *had* to come. I've run out of ideas and my mother is going to throw away my notebooks and . . . and I'll never be a writer!"

"Ahh . . ." said Miss Maddie. "We'd better have some tea."

When they got to the kitchen, Penelope sat down while Miss Maddie put on the kettle. After the stove was lit and the water was on, Miss Maddie joined her at the table. "So you've run out of ideas?" she asked.

"I thought my parents would give me more time to write if I could prove my stories were important," explained Penelope. "I have to write something good — something *amazing*. But my mind is blank. I can't come up with any-thing. I've tried for weeks and now it's too late. My mother wants to throw away my notebooks! I've been writing in those notebooks for years. They're my inspiration. Without them, I'll never come up with a story idea. Never!"

Miss Maddie pursed her lips and stared out the window. Penelope stared with her. Usually staring out the window made her feel relaxed, but not this time. The scenery outside looked flat, like the backdrop of a play.

Thwack! Miss Maddie slapped the table with her palm. Penelope sat up.

"Space!" she said.

"*Space?*" asked Penelope.

"Yes, yes. Space. Maybe your ideas are stuck. Maybe they got crowded out and all you need is a little bit of" — she fluttered her fingers around — "you know . . . space."

Space. It *sounded* like a good idea.

"Speaking of space," said Miss Maddie, "just how big is this hole in your schedule?"

Penelope took the calendar page from her pocket and smoothed it out on the table.

Miss Maddie leaned over. "That's pretty big," she said, tapping the calendar page with her finger.

Penelope nodded.

"Watch out," said Miss Maddie, "you could fall into a hole like that."

Penelope glanced up, expecting to see a twinkle in Miss Maddie's eye. But there was no twinkle. Or wink. Or even a smile. Miss Maddie was staring straight at her, a serious expression on her face. Just then the kettle screeched and Miss Maddie got up.

Penelope looked back down at the calendar page with Miss Maddie's words lingering in her mind. *You could fall into a hole like that . . .* Penelope noticed the white of the paper looked brighter than before, and the little black lines seemed faded. The longer she stared, the fainter the black lines grew, until they disappeared altogether. *That's odd*, thought Penelope. She blinked and gave her head a little shake. The lines reappeared.

Penelope looked over at Miss Maddie, who was spooning tea into the pot. "Tea will be ready in no time," Miss Maddie assured her.

Penelope nodded and stole another glance at the page. It happened again! The paper seemed to glow for a moment. Penelope looked closer. The lines were *definitely* growing fainter. *This time I'm not going to blink*, she decided.

Penelope kept her eyes open as wide as they would go. Sure enough, the white grew slowly brighter, and the black lines receded.

Don't blink, don't blink.

Penelope's eyes started to water, but she kept her resolve. The black lines had disappeared altogether and even the white seemed to fade into nothing.

Don't blink, don't blink.

Now the room disappeared. The only thing Penelope could see was the paper, which didn't even seem to be *there* anymore. Instead, a warm, white nothing opened out in front of her. Penelope felt like she was tottering at the edge of a pit. It made her feel queasy. So . . .

She blinked.

And in that brief moment of darkness, the pit rushed up. Or else she fell down. Either way, Penelope heard a whooshing sound and felt a strong wind press against her face. She opened her eyes and flung out her arms to brace herself against the table. But there *was* no table.

A jolt of panic sent Penelope's heart racing. Then the nothing engulfed her, and time slipped away into the rush of air.

chapter four

"Where did *you* come from?" said an unfamiliar voice.

Penelope turned her head in the direction of the sound. All she could see were little black dots dancing against a backdrop of brilliant light.

"Miss Maddie?" she called out.

"Who in the world is Miss Maddie?" the voice demanded.

Penelope squinted and the black dots slowed their dance. A shape wavered in front of her eyes, and she saw the outline of a face. She was lying on her back and a man was standing above her. The man had his hands on his knees and was inspecting her as if she were a beetle. He wore a pair of blue velvet pants and a matching velvet jacket covered in pockets. He seemed unusually tall, with legs as long as fence posts. His brilliant red hair stood straight up and should have made him look silly, except it didn't. Not quite. He looked old and wise and young and foolish all at the same time.

"Wh-where am I?" asked Penelope.

"The Realm of Possibility," the man answered matter-of-factly.

Penelope sat up. Her head was spinning and her back hurt. An uncomfortable lump in her pocket meant she'd landed on her notebook. "The realm of *what?*" she asked.

"The Realm of Possibility," repeated the man. "Used to be anything could happen here, but these days it rarely does. That's why you're so unusual. Bizarre. Highly irregular." He gave her arm a sharp poke, as if checking to see that she was real.

"Ow!" cried Penelope and glared up at him.

"Looks like you're here for good," said the man with a satisfied nod.

"But I can't be here for good," said Penelope, scrambling to her feet. "I have to be some-where else."

"Impossible."

Penelope gave the man a hard look. "What do you mean, 'impossible'?"

"I mean, you can't be somewhere else if you're already here. It's impossible. Inconceivable. Out of the question."

Penelope felt woozy. Her mother was going to kill her. Not only had she run away to Miss Maddie's, somehow she'd left town altogether! Penelope took a quick look around. She was standing on a small hill. Tall reeds swayed and hummed in the breeze. A well-worn dirt road ran down the hill to meet a field of stubby blue grass. To the right of the field, a forest of pine trees stood like sentries. There was not one house or street sign to be found. The woozy feeling moved from her stomach down to her knees.

Penelope turned back toward the man. "There *must* be a way out of here," she insisted.

But the man wasn't listening. "Do you see that?" he asked suddenly, pointing at the sky above the forest.

Penelope scanned the sky. It was empty except for a dark cloud huddled over the forest's far horizon. "You mean that cloud?" she asked.

When she looked back, the man was running headlong down the hill. "It looks like rain. I must be off!" he called over his shoulder. Once he reached the bottom of the hill, he left the road behind and took a trail through the grass heading straight for the forest.

"Wait!" Penelope shouted after him.

He stopped and turned around.

"I have to get back home! Can you please tell me where this road goes?"

"To the same place every day," he yelled back.

"But where *is* that?"

"If you don't know where you are, you can't possibly care where you're going. Now then, I really must go. Pleased to meet you."

"We *haven't* met!" shouted Penelope. But it was too late. The man had disappeared into the forest.

Penelope took a deep breath and tried to clear her head. *All you have to do is retrace your steps*, she told herself. But that was just it. Penelope didn't remember any steps. She had a vague memory of falling, but from where?

Penelope looked up. The rain cloud she had noticed earlier was moving swiftly across the sky. It didn't drift or roll like a cloud. It spread like a stain, smothering the sun and casting a gray light over the countryside. As the cloud drew closer, the soft breeze died away and the reeds stood still. The birds stopped singing and the bugs stopped twitching and a hush settled over the hill.

Penelope shuddered. Something didn't seem quite right about the cloud. In fact, something felt dreadful, though she couldn't tell what. Penelope's heart started to race and the next thing she knew she was running headlong down the hill in the same direction as the man.

As Penelope ran, she remembered all her mother's warnings about strangers. She considered her situation and decided that while the man certainly *seemed* strange in one way, he wasn't really the kind of stranger she was meant to avoid. Even so, the sooner she introduced herself the better. Then she would ask him for help. What choice did she have? There was no one else around.

Once Penelope reached the bottom of the hill, she veered off the road and onto the trail the man had followed into the forest. She plunged into the woods and the daylight immediately vanished under a thick canopy of shade. Trees crowded around her and tangled branches pressed in on every side. Penelope tried to push her way through the thick undergrowth, but soon lost the trail and with it, her sense of direction.

She heard humming up ahead and followed the sound, scanning the dim woods for a hint of red hair or a flash of blue suit. The humming sounded tantalizingly close, but the man was nowhere to be seen. Soon she was leaping over logs and brushing aside wisps of draping moss. And then, just like that, the humming stopped.

Penelope stood very still as the silence of the forest settled around her. She closed her eyes and held her breath, listening for some clue to the peculiar man's whereabouts. After a moment she heard a soft rustling sound like a mouse making its home. Penelope turned around in a slow circle, scanning the woods. That's when she saw it — a bit of red hair poking out from behind a tree. The man had left the path and was bending over a rotten stump, searching through a pile of decaying leaves.

"Hello?" called Penelope.

The man stood up immediately. "Mushrooms!"

"Wh-what?"

"Mushrooms!" he repeated, making his way toward her. He held out his hand. Two small, unassuming mushrooms sat on his palm. "You do like mushrooms, don't you?"

"They're . . . uh . . . they're very interesting," said Penelope, wishing she could say something intelligent based on what she'd learned at science camp.

The man beamed at her. "I couldn't agree with you more." He slipped the mushrooms into one of his many pockets. "That's settled, then. There's one for me and one for you. Of course, we'll have to wait until dinner."

"B-but I *can't* stay for dinner," stammered Penelope.

"Well, I suppose we could have them for an afternoon snack." He reached back into his pocket.

"You don't understand," she interrupted. "I don't have *time* to eat." Just then Penelope remembered her resolve to introduce herself. "My name is Penelope," she said, sticking out her hand. "And I'm from the Spicewood Estates."

"I'm Dill," he said with a quick shake.

"Like the pickle?" Penelope bit her lip. What a rude thing to say! She knew her mother wouldn't approve, but Dill didn't seem to mind. He smiled as if Penelope had compared him to someone famous.

"Exactly! Like the pickle."

Relieved, Penelope moved on to her request. "I was hoping you could help me. Do you know the way out of this Realm? I know you said it was impossible to leave, but if there's a way in, there must be a way out."

"I never said it was impossible to leave," replied Dill. "I said that if you're here, it's impossible to be anywhere else."

"Oh. So it *is* possible to leave?"

"Of course it's possible," said Dill.

Penelope went slack with relief. "Thank goodness."

"But highly unlikely," he continued.

Penelope suddenly felt very tired. They were going around and around and getting nowhere. She decided to change her approach. "Do you know *anyone* who knows the way out?"

The man frowned. "I suppose Chronos knows."

"*Who?*"

"Chronos." Dill fixed Penelope with a stare. "Ever heard of him?"

Penelope shook her head.

"Lucky you. He's unfriendly. Unpleasant. Actually" — his voice dropped to a whisper — "he's downright wicked."

"Wicked?" said Penelope, taking a step back. "I don't want to meet *him*."

"Indeed, you don't. It's best you stick with me for the time being. Now, I'd better get dinner started," he said, patting the pocket where he'd put the mushrooms. "These won't stay fresh for long."

Dill set off down the trail humming and Penelope hurried after so as not to be left behind. It sounded like she was stuck here, at least until she could figure out how to get home. Except she wasn't much good at figuring things out these days. Not with all her ideas dried up. She thought about poor Miss Maddie, who was probably trying to explain things to her mother at this very moment. Would her mother even *care* that Penelope was gone or would she just be upset that her schedule had been interrupted?

After walking for some time, they came to a clearing in the woods where a tiny sunlit meadow sat. The meadow was ringed by tall trees and topped with a bright blue sky.

"We're almost there!" Dill said and rushed ahead.

Penelope ran after him until — *bam!* — her foot hit something hard and she tumbled to the ground. She got to her feet, expecting Dill to reappear from around a tree or pop up from behind her. But he didn't. She looked left, then right. She looked up, then down. That's when she noticed what had tripped her — a stovepipe sticking up out of the dirt. A stovepipe meant there was a stove and a stove meant there was a kitchen and a kitchen meant . . . *aha!* There it was. A few feet from where she'd fallen was a door level with the ground. The door was open and Penelope peered through it down a deep hole to a pool of light below. Drifting up from the hole was the sound of banging cabinets and slamming drawers.

Penelope followed the noise down a ladder and soon arrived in a large open room fashioned from a cavern. The room had none of the dark dampness associated with caves. It was warm and brightly lit, with a living room on one end and a dining room on the other. The kitchen, where Dill was vigorously stirring something with a wire whisk, sat in the middle.

"Welcome! Greetings! Warmest salutations!" he called out to Penelope and nodded toward the living room. "Make yourself at home."

Penelope picked out a comfy-looking chair facing the kitchen and plopped down. The chair was carved out of a log and had pillows made from grape-colored moss. "Now then," said Dill, once Penelope was settled. "I'm dying to hear about these Spicewood Estates . . ."

"It's just a neighborhood," said Penelope with a shrug. "Lots of people live there."

"And there are spice woods?" he asked eagerly.

Penelope had often wondered about this. "No, there aren't any woods. Maybe there were at one time, but they're gone now. Mostly it's just houses."

"But these houses," pressed Dill, "they're beautiful estates with grounds and gardens?"

"It's not like that," Penelope insisted. "All the houses are the same with small yards."

Dill stopped stirring for a moment. "And you want to go back?"

"I *have* to go back," she explained. "I have a schedule to keep. Things I have to do. The longer I'm away, the farther behind I fall."

"I see." Dill resumed stirring. "I guess they're everywhere," he muttered.

Penelope sat up. "*Who's* everywhere?"

"I'd rather not say. There's no use ruining our appetite." Dill poured whatever he was making into a dish and slipped it into the oven. "I'll be right back. Just have to wash up a bit," he said and disappeared down the hall.

Penelope sat back in her chair and thought about Dill's question. *Did* she want to go back? She had no idea how she had gotten here, so she had no idea how to return. Maybe Dill would let her stay with him until she could come up with a plan. She couldn't help but wonder what she would be going back *to* anyway. By now her mother had probably thrown away all of Penelope's notebooks and was preparing to turn her room into an office.

Penelope got up from her chair to look around. The living room had two chairs and a long couch, each with the same grape-colored moss pillows. The pillows matched the wallpaper, which was every shade of purple imaginable — lavender, mauve, lilac, violet, plum, and wine. The most striking thing about the wallpaper wasn't the color, though. It was the texture. It was *bumpy*.

On closer inspection, Penelope realized the wallpaper wasn't wallpaper at all — it was mushrooms. Huge, spongy, purple mushrooms. Ebon and the other Mad Scientists would flip for these! Penelope reached out to touch one. Her fingertip disappeared in its fleshy exterior and then sprang back.

Bloop.

She couldn't resist doing it again.

Bloop. Bloop.

"Stop that!"

Penelope spun around, hands behind her back. Dill was striding toward her, his wild hair standing up even higher than usual. "Those mushrooms are *very* sensitive! They only grow under the most delicate conditions. You can't go around poking them!"

"I'm sorry," explained Penelope. "I didn't mean to hurt them."

Dill's eyes softened. "All right, then. They *are* hard to resist. They're awfully springy. Bouncy. Downright squishy."

"But what are they for?" asked Penelope.

"Eating, of course! Now then, if you please . . ." Dill escorted Penelope to the dining room and sat her at the head of the table, which was made from an enormous tree stump. He then retrieved a white dish from the kitchen. Spilling over the top of the dish was a gigantic lavender-colored soufflé. *"Bon appétit,"* he said in a hushed tone before placing it gently on the table.

"It looks delicious," said Penelope, who wasn't quite sure it did.

"Shh! You mustn't disturb it."

"Sorry," she whispered.

Dill rolled up his sleeves, took a large flat serving spoon, and approached the soufflé as if it were alive. He adjusted his angle several times before darting forward and swiftly tapping the soufflé along one of the many delicate creases across its top. When he did so, a puff of purple steam rose up and settled several feet above the dinner table.

Dill jumped on his chair and began to shovel bits of steam into his mouth with the serving spoon. "Quick! Grab your spoon!" he urged Penelope.

Penelope picked up her spoon and looked hesitantly at the purple cloud.

"You'll have to stand on your chair," said Dill, puffs of purple air escaping his mouth.

Penelope couldn't resist the idea of eating dinner standing on a chair, so up she went. The steam was thicker than expected and surprisingly easy to scoop up. Inside her mouth it swelled to twice its original size and then burst

into a series of delicate flavors: savory cream sauce, then toasted cheese, and finally vanilla ice cream with a tinge of hazelnut.

Neither of them said a word until the last bit of soufflé was gone. When they were finished, they sat down on their chairs with heavy sighs.

"That was amazing," said Penelope.

Dill let out a lavender-colored burp. "Thank you. I came up with the idea to make a soufflé so light you could only eat the steam, but I had the hardest time figuring out the recipe. The steam kept turning into soup in midair and causing the worst soggy mess. Or the soufflé was too light and only a mist would form. Have you ever tried to eat mist?"

Penelope shook her head.

"Well, I can tell you, it was a disaster. Failure. Total flop."

"What did you do?"

"I just kept moodling. I came up with hundreds of ideas. Most of them were too small, but I kept at it and after a while I moodled up a few big ones. With some tinkering, I turned those big ideas into real possibilities and from there I created my masterpiece — the lightest soufflé in the world!"

A faraway look crossed Dill's face and he stared past Penelope into a memory only he could see. "That was years ago. Years . . . and years . . . long before moodling was declared illegal . . ."

"What exactly *is* moodling?" interrupted Penelope, who was itching to add the word to her collection.

Dill leaned in as if sharing an important secret. "Moodling is daydreaming, letting your mind wander, losing track of time, and, in the most severe cases" — here he mouthed the words — "doing nothing."

Penelope's mouth dropped open. She did these things every chance she could! So did Miss Maddie! "What's so bad about letting your mind wander and . . . and . . . doing nothing?" she asked.

"I say, there's nothing wrong with a bit of moodling — you come up with the most interesting ideas that way. But you can only do it if Chronos isn't around. If he sees you, he'll send the Clockworkers to snatch you up and take you to the tower just like *that*." Dill snapped his fingers.

"Clockworkers!? Tower?" Penelope's voice was a high-pitched squeak.

"I can see it's time to tell you the story of the Great Moodler." Dill looked around the room quickly, as if they might not be alone. Once he seemed satisfied that no one was around, he continued, "Listen closely, but whatever you do, don't repeat a word. Your life just might depend upon it."

chapter five

THE STORY OF THE GREAT MOODLER

Once upon a time, so long ago I don't remember when, the Great Moodler was known far and wide for being exactly that — a *great* moodler. When most people moodle, they come up with a few ideas, but not the Great Moodler. She came up with real possibilities.

First she would moodle on the smallest, faintest notion. Soon it would blossom into an idea. With constant moodling, her ideas took flight, soaring overhead and colliding with one another until sparks flew. From the sparks, her ideas caught fire, streaking into the sky and exploding with possibilities.

In those days, possibilities fell to the ground like rain. Each one was a brilliant bit of light, etched with a message. "It's a possibility," people would say whenever they found one and, if they liked what it said, they'd pop it into their mouths and chew on it. Everyone was full of possibilities in those days — full to the point of bursting.

Most possibilities were quite ordinary, such as, ***Tomorrow it will rain.*** But some were intriguing and delicious, such as, ***There's a man in the moon*** or ***You can fly***. People loved these possibilities the most. Whenever someone discovered one, rather than chew

on it, they would sit right down and consider it. When they did, the possibility would grow. Sometimes it grew a little bit and sometimes a lot, but on the average most possibilities were about the size of a watermelon.

One night the Great Moodler had trouble sleeping. She got out of bed and stared up at the stars, moodling on the mysteries of life. When she did, a tiny possibility began to take shape. Even though it was very small, it was brighter and more beautiful than anything ever seen. It was like a sliver of the sun — so dazzling the night around it turned to day.

When the possibility took flight, people woke from their dreams and rushed outside to see what it was. They stared up in awe at the brilliant possibility, waiting for it to fall to the ground so they could consider it. But instead of falling, it streaked across the heavens like a meteor and disappeared from view.

Everyone was crushed. What was this possibility? What did it say? The very next day, explorers set out to find it. Because it was lost in some distant land, they called the treasure they were seeking the Remote Possibility. For years explorers trudged across deserts, slogged through swamps, and hacked their way through jungles, but the Remote Possibility was never found. One by one the explorers gave up their search and the Remote Possibility moved from memory into legend.

One explorer, though, never gave up. He climbed up the highest

mountains and down the deepest valleys in all four directions. When the Remote Possibility remained hidden, he searched harder and farther, traveling into the forgotten corners of the world.

One day while tramping through a rocky wasteland, surrounded by nothing but the dust and debris of a long-dead volcano, the explorer saw a glimmer on the ground up ahead. He was hungry and thirsty and his vision was blurred from exhaustion, but the light refused to fade. Was it a mirage? Or had he finally found what he'd been searching for?

Anything is possible, he told himself and pushed on toward the light. As he drew closer, the faint glimmer became a glow.

Anything is possible, he said again, putting one exhausted foot in front of the other. The light grew brighter still, turning the pebbles in its shadow into diamonds.

Once the treasure was finally within reach, the explorer bent down to pick it up. When he did, he let out a cry. For etched in the light were his very own words!

Anything is possible.

The explorer knew his search was over — the Remote Possibility had been found. He set off for home immediately, carrying his discovery with him. When he reached the border of the wasteland, he met a group of travelers. He shared the Remote Possibility with them, and as he did, the possibility began to grow. This in and of itself wasn't strange — that's what possibilities did. The strange thing was how *much* it grew. And grew. And grew. In just a matter of moments, it was the size of a bush, then a boulder.

"I can't believe it!" said one of the travelers.

"Anything is possible, I suppose," said another. And they all had to agree it was true. The proof was right in front of them.

By now the Remote Possibility was much too big for the explorer to carry, so he sent the travelers for help. But when help arrived, they had never seen a possibility so large and immediately began to consider it themselves. Of course, when they did, it grew even larger. Soon it was the size of a hill.

Word spread rapidly, and more and more people flocked to the wasteland. "Anything *is* possible," they would say when they saw the glittering mound of light. Up, up, up! The Remote Possibility grew bigger still until it was taller than the tallest mountain and wider than the sea.

By now the possibility was so large that people began to wonder what to do with it. Should they climb it? Dance around it? Chip it into pieces? They had no idea, but they knew someone who would — the Great Moodler.

The Great Moodler was a very gifted problem solver. It didn't matter if it was a big problem (like how to build a bridge to a rainbow) or a little problem (like how to catch a cricket), the Great Moodler would come up with a solution. But when she saw the Remote Possibility, even she was overwhelmed.

She moodled all day and all night. Hundreds of tiny notions streamed from her head and ideas bounced back and forth, but no real possibilities formed. So she moodled away the next day and the next night, too. Finally, after a week of almost constant moodling, a big idea began to take shape. Everyone held their breath, watching as she turned the idea this way and that. Suddenly it spun into the air and exploded with possibilities. The crowd cheered and the Great Moodler stood to announce her solution.

"This is what you must do with the Remote Possibility . . ." she shouted. The crowd grew silent, waiting for the answer.

"Live with it!"

Everyone was stunned. This wasn't the answer they were expecting. But the more they considered it, the more it made perfect sense. The Remote Possibility was so wonderful, so beautiful, they should build their lives around it. And that's what they did.

The Great Moodler quickly built a home on top of the gleaming mountain of light. She named the land in all four directions the Realm of Possibility. At the foot of the mountain, the people created a city that was beautiful beyond belief. The buildings were curvaceous and fanciful and went straight up into the clouds. The roads were long and winding and always followed the scenic route. People planted fruit trees along the highways to encourage musing and munching on the way to Wherever.

The city sat on one side of the Remote Possibility and the wasteland where it had been found sat on the other. The wasteland, however, was no longer a wasteland. The rocks and boulders bloomed in the light of the Remote Possibility and became grand mountains in their own right. But these mountains were no ordinary mountains. Instead of being brown or gray, like you might expect, they were blue, orange, green, pink, yellow — every color of the rainbow! People called them the Range of Possibilities and climbed their heights to reach the sun.

The Realm was a peaceful, beautiful place until one day a stranger came walking down the road. He carried nothing with him except a mysterious black book and a gold pocket watch. His name was Chronos and he had come to the Realm to make his mark. Chronos immediately built himself a giant home made of concrete and steel. He called his home, which was really more of a fortress, the Timely Manor. It held twenty-four rooms, one for each hour in the day. The rooms were dark and windowless and filled with ticking clocks. The outside walls were topped with a parapet where grim-faced Clockworkers marched day and night. No one knew exactly where the Clockworkers had come from, but one thing was sure — they lived to serve their master.

The Manor surrounded a central courtyard from which a tremendous clock tower rose. The tower had four clocks — one for each direction of the compass. Chronos was a proud man and he soon became jealous of the Great Moodler's place of importance. He believed the Realm was overrun with useless daydreamers and the Remote Possibility was nothing but a silly notion. He would often stand on the parapet and read aloud from his black book, shouting down to the people in the streets below. The book was filled with time-saving tips and words to live by, but most people ignored them. This made Chronos furious, so he came up with a plan.

In those days, the clock tower was a novelty, and no one paid it much mind. Everyone was too busy moodling to keep track of time. And why should they? There was time enough for everyone. People took as much as they needed and never worried about wasting it. Many had time to spare and would share it with anyone who asked. "There's no present like time," they'd say and give away minutes, hours, even days to those in need.

Chronos changed all that. Every day he ordered his Clockworkers to wind the clocks in the tower and every day, time would run out. People began to watch the clock, first out of curiosity and then in alarm. Time was slipping away. Soon people began to fight among themselves. "Take *your* time. Leave mine alone!" they argued. Neighbors accosted neighbors, demanding borrowed time back. What little time was left at the end of the day was heavily guarded lest it be stolen. It didn't take long before people turned to Chronos for answers. They gathered at the Manor and demanded an explanation. "Where has all the time gone?"

Chronos was prepared. "I'll tell you where it went," he roared, pointing to the Great Moodler's home on top of the Remote Possibility. "It's being wasted by that useless Moodler and by *you*!" This time he pointed an accusing finger at the crowd. "You are killing time with all your moodling. If you want more time, you must do as I say. Immediately!"

This got everyone's attention. "Killing time!" they said to one another. "How horrible. This must stop at once!"

They listened closely as Chronos explained his plan: "The more possibilities you consider, the less likely you are to accomplish anything. And the fewer things you accomplish, the more time you waste. Therefore, the quickest way to make the most of your time is to limit the possibilities." The people looked up at the clock tower in alarm. Sure enough, Chronos was right. Time was running out. There wasn't a minute to waste!

Chronos appointed twelve of his most efficient Clockworkers to a Committee devoted to making every second count. The first thing the Committee did was visit the Great Moodler and demand she stop coming up with new possibilities. "We have quite enough already!" they scolded her.

Next they decided to consider the possibilities they did have and throw out the ones that were a waste of time. After sifting through millions and millions of possibilities, they came up with a master list of 3,763. They passed an amendment to change *Anything is possible* to *3,763 things are possible*.

But they didn't stop there. Even *that* wasn't enough to save time, so they limited the possibilities even further, and as they did, the list became smaller . . .

2,631 . . . and smaller . . .

1,612 . . . and smaller . . .

497 . . . and smaller still . . .

Until it was decided: *217 things are possible*.

Anything struck from the list was deemed "Impossible" and declared illegal. Chronos established a court to prosecute time wasters and turned the

clock tower into a prison. With only 217 things possible, everyone knew *exactly* what they were supposed to be doing and when.

In gratitude for his efforts to save time, the Committee named the great city at the heart of the Realm after their leader. They called it Chronos City. Before long, the City outgrew its borders. As it grew bigger and bigger, it grew uglier and uglier. The Clockworkers shaved the ornamentation off the buildings, cut down the trees, and straightened the roads — all in the interest of efficiency.

The odd thing was, however, that no matter how much time people saved, there never seemed to be enough left over. The more things got done, the faster time ran out. Whether people were winding up or winding down, the clocks in the tower were always ticking. Soon the Realm was full of clocks. People carried them in their pockets, wore them on their wrists, and hung them on every wall. Before long, everyone's internal clock — the clock that told them when to do things in their own time — was completely drowned out.

"There's no such thing as an internal clock," scoffed Chronos. "Has anyone actually ever *seen* one?" People had to admit that no one ever had, whereas the clocks in the tower were undeniably real. Before long, people stopped even trying to check their internal clocks. They doubted they had ever *had* such a thing.

As doubt took hold in their minds, a dark Shadow gathered in the sky. At first it was nothing more than a mist hanging over the City, a slight haziness really. People hardly noticed it was there. But the more the clocks dictated people's every move — when to rise, when to eat, when to sleep — the darker the Shadow grew. The Shadow was darkest right above the tower, forming an impenetrable lid over the City. Before Chronos had arrived, every day had a rhythm, and the sun, moon, and stars kept the beat. Now there was no sun, moon, or stars to be seen. The Shadow had taken the place of the sky.

That's when the Great Moodler disappeared.

"High time!" said some who were glad to see her go.

"Better late than never," said others philosophically.

"It was only a matter of time," advised the Committee smugly.

Everyone had an opinion about where she'd gone. Some said she was banished. Others said she was lost in her own thoughts and couldn't find her way out. No one knew for sure. Either way, she was never seen again.

chapter six

"That's it? *That's* the story of the Great Moodler?" Penelope stared at Dill, willing him to continue.

Dill nodded. "That's it."

"Chronos took over and she disappeared?"

"Poof!" Dill waved his hands in the air. "Just like that."

"What about the Remote Possibility?" cried Penelope.

Dill shook his head sadly. "After the Great Moodler disappeared, the Remote Possibility shrank down to nothing. It hasn't been seen for ages."

Penelope sat in stunned silence. While listening to the story of the Great Moodler, a feeling of excitement had taken hold of her. The Great Moodler was an expert problem solver and a creative genius. If anyone could get her ideas flowing again, it was her! With her ideas back, Penelope could figure out how to make her dreams of being a writer come true. She could even figure out a way to get home, *if* she wanted to. Anything was possible!

But the Great Moodler was gone. And only 217 things were possible.

"I told you leaving was highly unlikely," continued Dill. "Now you know why. If Chronos knew you were here, he'd declare your arrival Impossible and whisk you away to the tower."

"I see what you mean," said Penelope in a daze.

Dill leaned across the table and gave her arm a gentle squeeze. "It's not so bad here. As long as we stay away from the City, we can moodle all we want. Besides, it sounds like your Spicewood Estates are overrun with Clockworkers."

Penelope gave him a weak smile. She couldn't bear to tell him the truth. Staying wasn't the problem. She *liked* it here. There was no daily schedule to follow or work-flow diagram to dictate her days. The problem was moodling. Maybe *Dill* could moodle all he wanted, but she couldn't. Her ideas were stuck. And with the Great Moodler gone, they were likely to stay that way.

"Dill?" said Penelope, her heart caught in her chest. "Have you ever tried to find the Great Moodler?"

Dill's shoulders slumped and his eyes glistened with what looked like tears. "Of course I've tried! I was looking for her when I bumped into you. I've moodled for days, weeks, months. I can't come up with a single idea, much less a real possibility as to where she is. I'm afraid it's hopeless. Useless. Absolutely futile."

Penelope thought about all the bad story ideas she'd come up with in the last few weeks and the blank wall her mind had eventually become. She knew exactly how he felt.

"I don't know what happened," said Dill, wiping his eyes with a handkerchief. "I used to be a great explorer. I could find anything — absolutely *anything*."

He glanced up at Penelope with a wry smile. "I was the one who found the Remote Possibility, you know."

Penelope's mouth dropped open. "You *were?*"

"Oh, yes. Distant memories, buried dreams, lost hopes — I found them all. I was a real hero in those days. You should have heard the people cheering when I came back from an expedition. But that's all over now. Exploring has been declared a waste of time and therefore Impossible by decree of Chronos. I haven't found anything in ages." Dill sighed a deep, unhappy sigh. He stared down at the floor, his shoulders still hunched. A moment later, he popped up and stared at Penelope, as if seeing her for the very first time. "Maybe *you* could give it a try."

Penelope glanced around. "Give *what* a try?"

Dill ignored her question. "Don't go anywhere. I'll be right back . . ." He rushed out of the room and soon returned with a small, shiny object.

"What is it?" asked Penelope.

"It's a moodle hat." Dill gave the hat a quick snap of the wrist and the top popped up. It was shaped like a bowl with a flat rim about three inches wide. He handed the hat gently to Penelope, who examined it. It was made of some sort of silvery mesh material. "How does it work?" she asked.

Dill leaned forward, his eyes practically glowing. "Now *that* is a very good question. On the outside, it looks ordinary. Unremarkable. Extremely plain. But on the inside, it couldn't be more fantastic. The lining is full of very small, very sophisticated traps — sticky snatchers, grabby gadgets, spring-loaded snappers — the works!"

Penelope peered under the hat to see the traps.

"You can't *see* anything," explained Dill. "It's all microscopic. You'll never guess what the traps do. Never, *ever*. So, I'll just have to tell you. They trap ideas, Penelope! All those glorious ideas, streaming and bubbling out of your head, all the ideas you couldn't keep ahold of, until . . . *snap!*" He flung his arms open wide, then slammed his hands together. "The moodle hat traps them for good!

"Imagine!" said Dill, walking wildly about. "The biggest, fattest, grandest ideas are all yours and the skinny, scrawny ones escape into the stratosphere, where they can fatten up a bit before dropping down and lodging in someone else's head." Dill spun around to face her. "Without this hat I never would have found the Remote Possibility. And now you can use it to find the Great Moodler!"

"*Me?*" squeaked Penelope.

"Yes, *you*. Ever since Chronos took over and the Great Moodler disappeared, I've felt lost. And how can I find anyone, if I can't find myself? But *you*," said Dill, giving Penelope's arm a little shake, "you might be able to moodle up an idea of where she went."

Dill looked so hopeful, Penelope couldn't bear to tell him that there was no chance of her coming up with a little idea, much less a big one. "You go first," she said, stalling for time. "To show me how it's done."

"All right." Dill took the hat and put it on. He hurried over to the couch and lay down, propping his head up on the armrest. "Hmmm . . ." he said, tapping his cheek with a long finger, "where is the Great Moodler?"

Penelope sat down on a moss-covered chair to watch. Her feet dangled to the floor and she tapped them nervously. *Tap. Tap. Tap.* There was no way she would be of any help. *Tap. Tap. Tap.* She might come up with a few lame fantasies, but she was all out of good ideas. Dill was sure to be disappointed. *Tap. Tap. Tap.*

Dill glared at her.

"Sorry," she mouthed.

Penelope sat as still as she could, almost not daring to breathe, and waited. After a while, Dill closed his eyes and Penelope thought he had fallen asleep. But every once in a while he'd scrunch his mouth or tweak his nose and the waiting would continue. Watching someone do nothing made Penelope sleepy and soon her head began to dip and sway in a lazy arc. *Snap!* She yanked herself back to attention. But her head dipped again . . . and again. Before long she lost the struggle and fell into a light sleep, her head resting on her chest.

"Drat! Fiddlesticks! Gosh darn it all!"

Penelope jerked awake. "What's wrong?" she asked, trying to sound alert.

"I don't have any ideas," said Dill. "None. Zero. Absolute zilch! It's just like before."

"Try staring out a window," offered Penelope.

"I don't have any windows," grumbled Dill. He took off the hat and held it out to Penelope. "Here, you try. My mind is blank."

Penelope knew the feeling all too well. She took the hat and held it in her lap for a moment. "What am I supposed to do again?" she asked.

"You don't *do* anything," insisted Dill. "If you do something you'll muck it all up. Just let your mind wander and the hat will capture any big ideas. But don't think too hard. And absolutely no analyzing, cogitating, or figuring of any kind."

Penelope slowly raised the hat up to her head. *There's no way this is going to work*, she said to herself. *I'm all out of ideas. I don't know what I'm doing. I hope Dill won't be mad and —*

Penelope's last thought was cut off as she lowered the hat onto her head. She heard, or rather felt, a soft *whir-whir.*

"Now, ask yourself where the Great Moodler is," whispered Dill. "But remember, no thinking! Just let your mind go."

Penelope tried to concentrate on the question while at the same time not thinking. It felt like she was trying to open a door and shut it at the same time. Sometimes a thought floated by — *I wonder what the Great Moodler looks like* or *My foot is falling asleep.* But for the most part, nothing came to mind. Penelope stared at the nothing. It was bright and beautiful. Somehow it made her feel peaceful.

Whir-whir-whir . . . The longer she stared at the nothing, the faster the whirring sound went.

Does the whirring mean it's working? she wondered. *If so, where are all the ideas?*

Penelope let these thoughts slip away and for a minute (or was it an hour?) she slipped away with them. Just then she felt a *snap.* It vibrated through her body and brought her back to reality. She opened her eyes.

Dill was staring at the hat. "That's really something," he said in a hushed voice.

Penelope slowly lowered the hat from her head. It had grown! The silvery mesh material had stretched to the size of a beach ball. Something like a huge bubble struggled to get out. And then — *pop!* — just like that, it disappeared.

Dill turned quickly to Penelope. "So what's the big idea?" he demanded.

Penelope shrugged. "I — I don't know."

"You mean, nothing came to mind?"

"Nothing," said Penelope.

"Nothing? Like nil? *Nada?* Diddly-squat?"

Penelope nodded.

Dill's shoulders sagged. "Oh, well. I suppose the bubble is just an anomaly. We'll try again in the morning."

Penelope wondered what *anomaly* meant. She decided it must be another word for failure.

chapter seven

After the soufflé dish and silverware were washed and put away, Dill escorted Penelope down a long hall, stopping before a door made of dark wood. Inside was a bed made from the roots of a tree growing directly overhead. The roots, which extended down into the room, had been coaxed into the shape of a large, intricately woven basket. The bed, or basket, as it were, was piled ridiculously high with pillows and blankets.

"Sleep well," said Dill.

"Good night," said Penelope and closed the door.

Penelope sat down on the edge of the bed and took out her notebook. She added *moodle* to her list of fascinating words. She also added *anomaly*. Next to *anomaly*, she wrote the word *failure* and a question mark. Afterward, she jotted down the important moments of her day — the hole in her schedule, meeting Dill, the story of the Great Moodler — before slipping off her shoes and crawling under the covers.

The bed rocked back and forth ever so slightly as if the tree above her was swaying in the breeze. The gentle movement should have put Penelope right to sleep, but it didn't. Instead, she lay there thinking about her mother. When her mother had a problem, she got organized. But Penelope wasn't very good at coming up with schedules, action items, and agendas. The only thing she was any good at was moodling, and now she was even a failure at that!

Why can't I come up with any ideas?

Where did they all go?

Penelope rolled over onto her side and squeezed her eyes shut, trying to clear her head.

If I can't come up with any ideas, I'll never find the Great Moodler.

Dill will be so disappointed.

Penelope sat up. She punched her pillow a few times, then lay back down. But as soon as she closed her eyes, the worries started streaming in.

I'll moodle and moodle and nothing will happen . . .

Pop.

Except Chronos will probably catch me . . .

Pop-pop.

And send me to the clock tower!

Penelope was so consumed with the process of worrying that she hardly noticed a very soft popping sound coming from nearby.

I'll starve in the tower or catch pneumonia . . .

Pop-pop.

Or turn into a Clockworker . . .

Pop-pop-pop.

And never be a writer!

Poppity-pop-pop.

Each new worry spawned another worry. And another. Soon they were coming so fast Penelope couldn't keep up. She tossed and turned late into the night. It wasn't until she fell into a fitful sleep that the worries ceased and the popping grew silent.

-- -- --

Penelope woke before dawn to the smell of burnt toast. After stumbling around a bit, she managed to find her notebook and shoes, then made her way to the kitchen.

"Good morning! Ready for . . ." Dill's voice trailed off. He put down the honey jar he was holding and hurried toward Penelope. "Did you sleep all right?"

"Not really," she said, stifling a yawn. "I stayed up half the night worrying about finding the Great Moodler."

"I can see that." Dill took Penelope by the shoulders, turning her this way and that. "It's written *all over* your face."

Penelope put a hand up to her cheek and gasped. She felt bumps. She touched her forehead, nose, and chin. Bumps, bumps, and more bumps. "What happened to me?" she cried.

Dill gripped her shoulder. "I'll tell you on one condition."

"Okay," said Penelope, her heart racing.

"You have to promise me not to worry."

If Penelope hadn't been so dazed, she might have protested. Instead, she limply crossed her heart. "I promise."

Dill dragged Penelope over to the living room and sat her down. He turned to a cabinet nearby and took out a mirror, holding it against his chest. "Remember, you promised not to worry."

Penelope nodded and held out her hand. Dill gave her the mirror.

She immediately forgot her promise. Her face was covered with bumps — wrinkly red bumps. "I have a disease!" she screamed, and right before her eyes — *pop, pop, pop* — three more appeared on her nose.

"*You promised not to worry!*" shrieked Dill and snatched the mirror away.

Penelope snatched it right back. "How can you tell me not to worry? I've got bumps all over my face!"

"Those *aren't* bumps. They're worry warts. If we had a magnifying glass you'd see they're made of teeny-tiny words spelling out your troubles. The more you worry, the worse they get."

Penelope wasn't listening. She was staring at her reflection. *I'm going through the rest of my life covered in ugly red warts*, she thought. *I'll never be able to show my face in public again!* A few more warts squeezed onto her forehead — *Pop! Pop!* Her face was in danger of disappearing altogether.

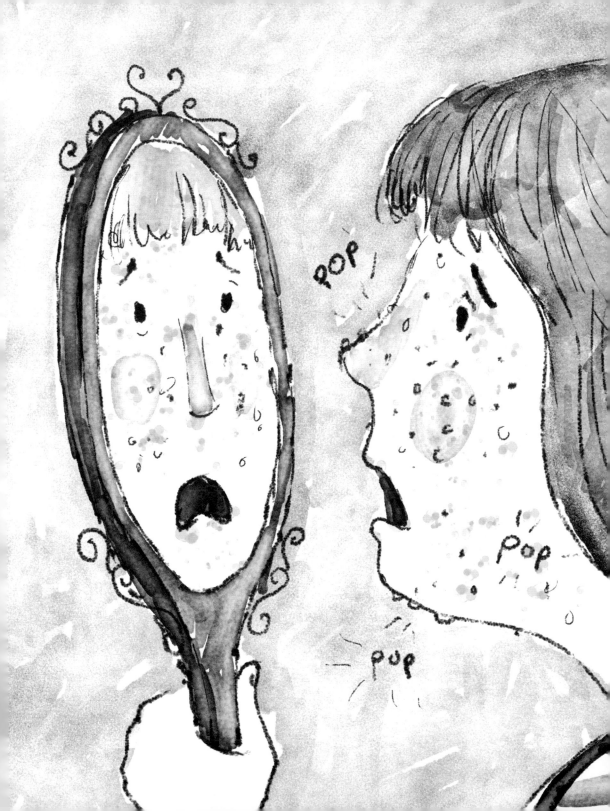

Dill knelt down beside Penelope. "Quick! Tell me what you were worried about."

Penelope dragged her eyes away from the mirror and tried to focus.

"Please," pleaded Dill. "It's important you remember."

Penelope closed her eyes and tried to make a list. "Being captured by Chronos . . . wasting away in the tower . . . catching pneumonia . . . starving to death . . ." She peeked out of one eye.

"Go on, go on," urged Dill.

Penelope took a deep breath and let the words rush out. "Turning into a Clockworker and never moodling again!"

"Horrible, horrible, horrible!" Dill leapt to his feet and began to run around, snatching things from closets and cabinets — bits of rope, flashlights, boots, and hammers.

"Imprisonment! Starvation! Pneumonia!" He dashed off to the next room and came charging back with several boxes of tissues, which he threw onto the growing pile.

"We're almost ready now," he said and disappeared into the hall closet.

"Ready for what?" asked Penelope.

Dill emerged from the closet, holding a stepladder and an inflatable raft. "What do you *mean*, 'for what?' We've got a lot of disastrous matters to take care of."

Penelope scrunched down in her chair. "Not really," she said. "Nothing *actually* happened."

Dill dropped the stepladder. "Nothing?"

Penelope shook her head.

"*Absolutely* nothing?"

Penelope shook her head again.

"You're telling me, you stayed up half the night for no good reason?"

"I had plenty of reasons!" insisted Penelope. "You saw me try the moodle hat. I'm useless. I'll never be able to help you find the Great Moodler or fend off Chronos and his Clockworkers if they find out I'm here."

"Worrying won't change all that. By the way, I think they're spreading," said Dill, pointing at her neck.

Penelope checked. Sure enough, there were more bumps. "What am I going to do?" she cried.

"Stop worrying. They're bound to go away."

"*When?*" Penelope demanded.

Dill's muffled voice came from inside the closet, where he was busily putting away everything he'd just taken out. "It should only take a few hours . . . or a few days."

"A few *days?*" Penelope couldn't believe what she was hearing.

Dill popped out of the closet and tried shoving it closed with his shoulder. "To be honest," he said, huffing and puffing, "I have no idea how long it will take. I've never had worry warts myself, so I'm not sure what the cure is."

"*You don't know what the cure is?*" POP! POP! POP! Penelope's face and neck erupted in a fury of red bumps.

"Nope," said Dill and gave the door a final shove. There was a muffled crash before it clicked obediently closed.

"Can't you think of something?" Penelope pleaded.

"Well," said Dill, drumming his fingers on his chin. "I can certainly give it a try."

Penelope watched him, holding her breath, trying not to worry.

"Pirates!" Dill suddenly shouted.

Penelope looked around quickly. "Where?"

"Not *here*," said Dill. "Last night, in your worries. Did they show up?"

"No . . ."

"How about tigers? Did you worry about them?"

"Of course not. That's ridiculous."

Dill flung open his arms. "There you have it!"

"What do I have?" Penelope said each word very carefully. She was fighting the urge to throw the mirror at him.

"The cure!"

Penelope looked at her reflection. The worry warts hadn't gone any-where. "*What* are you talking about?" she practically screamed.

"If you got the warts by worrying about all the bad things that *could* have happened, then the best way to get rid of them is to think about all the bad things that *couldn't* have happened. It's like worrying, but in reverse."

Penelope stared at Dill, her eyes bulging. *Who ever heard of worrying in reverse?*

"Here, let me help," he continued. "What's your least favorite thing?"

"Snakes," she answered immediately. That was an easy one.

"Well, then," urged Dill, "tell me something about snakes that couldn't possibly have happened last night."

Penelope thought about it for a moment. "I didn't get squeezed to death by a python?" It was really more of a question.

"You're a very lucky girl," said Dill, his voice deep and serious.

Penelope thought she might have felt a slight tingling sensation in her face. Either the worrying in reverse was working, or she was just embarrassed.

"Go ahead," prompted Dill. "What's another awful thing you didn't have to worry about?"

"I didn't fall into a pit."

"Or get snapped in two by sharks," Dill added helpfully.

Penelope couldn't help but giggle. "Or swept away by a dust storm . . ."

"Or drowned in a whirlpool. Or run over by an elephant."

"Or frozen inside a glacier!"

By now Penelope's cheeks were burning hot, but she kept going. "I didn't get captured by headhunters . . ."

"Or eaten by cannibals . . ."

"Or thrown into a bed of scorpions!"

"It's working!" shouted Dill, pointing at her face.

Penelope held up the mirror, turning it this way and that. She watched as the last remaining wart faded from bright red to soft pink to the same creamy color as her skin. Then, just like that, it was gone.

"Congratulations!" said Dill, giving Penelope's hand a firm shake. "It's official. You've got nothing to worry about."

chapter eight

Penelope sank back into her chair with relief. The heat from her face melted away, flooding her body with a warm, relaxed feeling. So this was what it felt like to have nothing to worry about.

"Up, up, up!" demanded Dill, clapping his hands.

Penelope, who had just been contemplating going back to bed, didn't budge.

"We've got a sunrise to catch," he insisted. "You don't want to miss it."

Penelope dragged herself to her feet. She followed Dill down the front hall, up the ladder, and out into the cool dark of early morning. But instead of a sun peeking through the trees, they were met by a stark gray sky.

"That's strange," said Dill. "The sun should be here by now."

"Maybe we're up too early." Penelope stifled a yawn. "Maybe it's actually still nighttime."

"If it's nighttime, then where are the stars? No, no, no. Something is definitely wrong. Awry. Out of order."

Penelope looked at the sky. She suddenly felt an odd chill that had nothing to do with the temperature. It seemed to come from her own bones. She remembered the rain cloud Dill had pointed out yesterday and how it had continued to move even after the wind had grown still. How it had blackened the sky and filled her with dread. She felt that same dread now.

Dill must have felt it, too. He turned to Penelope, his face white. "We've got to go. They'll be here soon. Swarms of them."

"Swarms of *what?*" asked Penelope, suddenly awake.

"Clockworkers. That's no cloud," he said, pointing upward. "That's the Shadow."

"The Shadow from Chronos City?" Penelope couldn't believe what she was hearing. "What's it doing *here?*"

"I have no idea, but whatever the reason, it can't be good. We've *got* to get out of here until it passes." Dill hurried back down the ladder and Penelope scrambled after him.

"Where will we go?" she asked as Dill flung odds and ends into a backpack.

"The mountains." Dill's voice was grim, his jaw clenched. "I know a short-cut through the woods to the Range of Possibilities. We'll be halfway there before the Clockworkers reach my meadow. But only if we act fast." He began rifling through drawers and stuffing his many pockets with provisions.

"What about finding the Great Moodler?" Despite all her worries, Penelope wasn't ready to abandon her search.

"The Great Moodler will have to wait." Dill hoisted the pack over his shoulder. "We'll never find her if we're imprisoned in the clock tower. Now *come on.*"

Once outside, Dill and Penelope took off across the meadow. Penelope practically had to run to keep up with Dill's long strides. When they reached the far end of the clearing, a wild, overgrown hedge blocked their way. An ancient wooden sign pointed directly at the impenetrable mass of bushes and brambles. Penelope could just make out the words:

THIS WAY TO THE NAUGHTY WOULDS.

She stifled a laugh. "Shouldn't that say, 'This way to the *Knotty Woods*'?"

Dill looked at the sign and then back at Penelope. "That's *exactly* what it says. 'This way to the Naughty Woulds.'"

"No, it says, 'naughty,' but woods aren't naughty, they're 'knotty.' And what are 'woulds'? I've never heard of such a thing."

"Well, you have now." Dill walked up to the sign and gave it a heave. "Help me out, will you? No use telling the Clockworkers which way we've gone." Together they were able to pull the sign out of the ground. Once they'd hidden it under a bush, Dill found a shrub peppered with little red berries and pulled back one of its branches.

"After you," he said with a quick bow.

Penelope leaned forward. A dark tunnel opened out in front of her. Thorny brambles crowded the tunnel as if trying to take it back, and a dank, musty smell filled the air. A path ran forward a few feet and then, with a sharp twist, disappeared.

"Are you *sure* this is the right way?" she asked, looking up at Dill.

"Of course I'm sure! Going around the Woulds takes days and days. If we want to stay ahead of the Clockworkers, there's nothing to do but go through them."

"Maybe you should go first," said Penelope.

"All right, then." Dill stepped inside and Penelope followed. Once they were both inside, he let the branch drop. What little light there was vanished and the air suddenly seemed to thicken. "I recommend you stay on the path," whispered Dill. "You don't want to go wandering around."

"Don't worry," Penelope whispered back. "I won't."

They set off together through the tunnel. Penelope had to hunch down in order to pass, while poor Dill was practically doubled over at the waist. Branches caught their sleeves and hair like long fingers, and they often had to stop and untangle themselves.

Even though the hedge seemed determined to block their path, it eventually opened out into an ancient forest packed with trees. Gnarled branches drooped down across their way and moss hung from every surface. Faint strips of dusty light illuminated the path, which was nearly hidden under a carpet of decaying leaves.

Dill led the way through the woods, humming and pointing out patches of mushrooms growing here and there. Some were light with dark spots, others were dark with light spots, but most were a dull yellow color with strange, fleshy warts. A very few were a translucent white with bright orange underneath. These were Penelope's favorites, but Dill cautioned her against touching them.

"Those will give you an incurable case of the hiccups," he said and then returned to his humming.

Every so often Dill would stop to examine the mushrooms and once or twice he plucked a smaller whitish one, tucking it into one of the pockets covering his jacket. "Just a little something for later," he explained. "Ever tried mushroom-and-halibut goulash?"

"No," said Penelope, hoping she never would.

"How about acorn-and-mushroom pâté?"

"No."

"Mushroom loaf with horseradish sauce?"

"No."

"Pickled mushrooms with prunes?"

"Definitely not!"

Dill shook his head. "You don't know what you're missing."

"How do you know so much about mushrooms?" Penelope asked.

"How come you know so little?"

"I never paid attention to them, even in science camp when I was supposed to. I thought they were gross," admitted Penelope.

"Mushrooms are *not* gross. They're wonderful. Fabulous. Absolutely marvelous. Back when I was searching for the Remote Possibility, I would have starved if it weren't for mushrooms. No matter where I was, I could find a mushroom or two to eat. When I returned from my adventure, I decided to grow them myself. That's why I've come up with so many recipes. I could eat mushrooms for breakfast, lunch, and . . ." Dill suddenly stopped and his voice dropped to a whisper. "Do you see what I see?"

Penelope lowered her voice as well. "What?"

"There! Look at the foot of that tree. The big one, far in the distance."

Penelope could see a cluster of tall, thin trees to her right. Beyond them stood an ancient oak with a trunk as big around as a house. Something glowed faintly among the oak's huge roots. "What are those glowing things?" she asked.

"Mushrooms. Very rare, very delicious mushrooms. Stay right where you are. I'll be back." Dill stepped off the path and darted through the trees.

"Where are you going?" Penelope called out after him.

"To pick them, of course!"

Penelope watched as Dill skipped over the fallen branches and snaking roots that covered the ground. Just before he reached the great tree, he stopped and looked over his shoulder. "I almost forgot," he yelled at Penelope. "Whatever you do, keep up the humming until I get back." Dill stepped behind the tree's giant trunk and was gone.

Penelope pondered his instructions. What was so important about humming? She tried humming a few bars of "Yankee Doodle." When she did, she felt the silence of the forest push against her, and her humming grew softer and softer until it died away altogether. A hush settled around her like a heavy blanket, pressing against her chest. At that moment, Penelope heard, almost imperceptibly, something that sounded like whispering. She strained to listen. There it was — voices in the distant background. Penelope scanned the forest, trying to locate the source of the sound, but all she saw were trees. They loomed over her, backs hunched, leaves limp.

Penelope closed her eyes and listened harder. The voices grew louder. The whispering was more like murmuring now. It seemed to be coming from directly above her. Penelope opened her eyes and thought she saw a slight movement in the branches, but couldn't be sure. She suddenly had the feeling she was being watched.

That's when the voices started in earnest.

The first voice was raspy and high-pitched, like the sound of an old woman. "Wouldn't it be better if she weren't such a scatterbrain?" it cackled.

"Wouldn't it be better if she were smarter?" said a second voice, much like the first.

"Wouldn't it be better if she were more organized?" chimed a third.

"Wouldn't it be better if she were more efficient?" said the fourth.

"It would! It would!" they all exclaimed together.

Penelope stood very still, listening. Were the voices talking about *her*? She looked back up at the trees. There it was again! That little flicker of movement that disappeared when it caught her eye.

"I think we can *all* agree," said the fourth voice, louder than before, "that if she weren't such a scatterbrain, she would be more productive . . ."

"She would be more useful . . ."

"She would be more successful . . ."

"She would be more competitive . . ."

Penelope's mouth dropped open. They *were* talking about her! But who, exactly, were *they*? She felt a sharp branch — or was it a finger? — graze her back. Penelope whirled around. There wasn't anything there — except a tree. Was it closer than before? She heard a snickering sound behind her and spun back to face the way she'd come. The tree in front of her was closer, too! All of the trees looked like they were leaning over her, pushed by a strong wind. Except there *was* no wind. The air was perfectly still.

Just then, the voices started again. This time they were screaming.

"If I were you, I would be ashamed of myself!"

"I would be embarrassed to show my face in public!"

"I would never leave the house!"

Penelope tried to run away, pushing against the branches that now blocked her path. In an instant the earth shifted underneath her and several long, dark roots crept up and around her feet. She kicked at them and they recoiled only to snap back and wrap tightly around her ankles. Once Penelope was anchored to the ground, a thin layer of moss sprouted over her shoes and began to move up her legs.

The voices were laughing now — a horrible screeching sound. Penelope brushed desperately at the moss, trying to knock it away, but it only crept higher. Penelope's knees buckled and she slid to the ground. When she did, the roots leapt up and wrapped around her wrists. Penelope tried to pull her hands free, but the roots were too strong. They held her down as the moss moved around her waist, creeping higher and higher with each second.

Penelope squeezed her eyes closed, fighting back tears. Screams and cheers ricocheted through the forest, until . . .

"Hush!"

Penelope's eyes snapped open. Dill was standing over her, shaking his fists at the trees. "Mind your own business! You're nothing but a bunch of bullies!" he shouted.

To Penelope's complete surprise, the trees fell silent and slowly began to melt back into the forest. Their roots, which had so firmly grasped Penelope, recoiled from her wrists and ankles.

Dill knelt down beside her. "Are you all right?" he asked.

"I — I think so," she stammered.

Dill helped Penelope to her feet and began brushing moss and leaves from her clothes. "The trees are really quite pathetic. If you stand up to them, they'll just go away. If you don't, they'll ensnare you in their chatter. *Wouldn't it be better if she were this, wouldn't it be better if she were that?* Those woulds are troublesome. Nasty. Very naughty."

"So *that's* what you meant by 'Naughty Woulds'!" said Penelope with a shaky laugh. "Now I understand. Why didn't you warn me?"

"I didn't want you to worry," said Dill. "And, really, there's nothing to worry about."

"There's *not?* How do you keep them from trapping you?"

"Humming!" declared Dill, pointing up at the sky as if leading a charge.

"*Humming?*" Penelope could hardly believe what she was hearing. Humming seemed like such a slight defense against the Naughty Woulds.

"Humming drives away the trees. They can't catch you if you're listening to your own tune," he explained.

Penelope thought about the horrible roots that had gripped her legs and arms. They had almost trapped her! She shook the memory loose and looked at Dill. "And . . . and what if you *don't* listen to your own tune?" she asked softly.

Dill pointed to a large moss-covered rock on the path ahead. "See for yourself."

Penelope approached the rock slowly. On closer inspection, she could see it wasn't a rock at all. She could just make out a hunched figure, anchored to the ground by moss, its features turned to stone.

"That's a person!" cried Penelope.

"Indeed it is," said Dill, joining her alongside the figure.

"But what happened to him?"

"He listened to the trees and believed them."

Penelope took a step back. *So did I*, she thought, her heart thumping.

Dill must have read her mind. He put one long arm around her shoulders and gave her a quick squeeze. "What are friends for, if they can't help keep the Naughty Woulds at bay? After all, who can say how you *would* be if things were one way or another? All we know is how you are, and how you are is exactly how you're meant to be."

Penelope stared up at Dill. He made it sound so simple. The way she was, was exactly how she was meant to be. It was the Naughty Woulds that were twisted and flawed. Her heart slowed its thumping and she smiled. Dill smiled back and then adjusted his coat with a brisk tug. "Ready?" he asked.

"Ready," said Penelope.

Dill set off down the trail humming. This time Penelope joined in.

chapter nine

Once they reached the edge of the Naughty Woulds, Dill and Penelope burst out of the trees and into the day. They were standing on a high, rocky ridge. A long valley of waving blue grass opened out below them. Above them, a bright open sky hung dotted with clouds. They stood for a moment, taking in the view and letting the memory of the dark woods fade.

Dill pointed to a boulder soaking up the sun. "That's a perfect place for a picnic." Penelope agreed and together they climbed onto the rock and settled on the side facing the valley with the Woulds behind them. Dill took out the glowing mushrooms he'd picked in the forest. He popped the cap off one and handed it to Penelope. "Eat it quick or the glow will fade," he urged.

Penelope put it in her mouth. When the mushroom touched her tongue it dissolved, leaving behind a taste that could only be described as *warm*. The warm slipped down her throat and into her stomach, filling her whole body with its glow.

Dill and Penelope sat in silence, savoring the heavenly mushrooms. After a moment, Dill let out a gigantic yawn. "These mushrooms always make me sleepy. Wake me up in five minutes, would you?" He lay back and closed his eyes. In a matter of seconds, Dill's breathing dropped to a slow rhythm and he was asleep. Penelope slipped out her notebook. She might not have any ideas, but at least she would have memories. She wrote about the worry warts and the Shadow and the Naughty Woulds and all the amazing mushrooms she'd seen. She lost track of time, letting it slip away in the stream of words. She didn't stop writing until she was startled by the sound of Dill's snoring. She stuffed her notebook in her pocket and gave him a gentle shove. "Wake up," she urged, hoping five minutes hadn't already passed.

Dill sat up and stretched. "I guess we'd better get going." A sudden frown crossed his face and he pointed back toward the direction they had come. "Will you look at that?" he said, scrambling to his feet. "The Clockworkers have already reached my meadow."

Penelope followed his gaze. From their position high upon the ridge, the Naughty Woulds stretched out behind them. Sure enough, the sky on the far side of the forest looked heavy and dark.

Dill grabbed his pack. "I doubt they'll push on through the Naughty Woulds with evening so close, but still, we'd better get going." He climbed down the boulder and offered Penelope a hand. She took it and jumped down to the ground.

"What do the Clockworkers want with your meadow anyway?" she asked.

Dill shrugged. "It's a mystery. Puzzle. Complete conundrum. They're always on the lookout for time wasters or moodlers, so maybe . . ."

"Maybe they're onto us. . . ." said Penelope, her heart pounding. "Maybe they know I'm here."

Dill looked at Penelope. Penelope looked at Dill. They both nodded. "Let's get going."

Dill turned back toward the valley and pointed to a row of trees on the far side. "Beneath those trees there's a creek we must cross, and beyond that are the foothills of the Range of Possibilities. With luck we'll be in the mountains for dinner."

They scrambled down the ridge and followed a dirt path that zigzagged through the valley. Little white flowers were scattered throughout the deep grass. The blossoms seemed to perk up and salute them as they passed. Dill bobbed his head in greeting to this flower or that. Whenever they reached a clump of bushes or a large rock, he came to a halt and motioned for Penelope to do the same. Then he would peer under the bush or around the rock as if it were hiding something.

"Are you looking for mushrooms?" asked Penelope.

"No," whispered Dill. "Wild Bore."

"Wild boar?" Penelope looked around the sunny, flower-filled pasture. "*Here?*"

Dill waved at her to be quiet. "Keep your voice down. You never know where they might be lurking. It's important to be on guard. They like to sneak up on people."

Penelope imagined a large hairy pig with tusks tiptoeing after them. She fought back the urge to giggle. "How do they sneak up on people?" she whispered, trying to sound serious. "Don't they make a lot of noise grunting and snorting?"

"Oh, no," insisted Dill. "They're very sneaky. And fast. If you get caught by one, don't even bother running. Your only hope is to see it coming."

"What do you do if you see one?"

"Start talking. If you say the first word, they'll leave you alone. If you don't, your only hope is to get a word in edgewise. That usually stops them cold. If you can't do *that* . . ." Dill shook his head. "Let's just say, it's best not to get caught in the first place."

"Got it," said Penelope. But she wasn't sure she did. What good would it do to talk to a pig? Wouldn't it just be better to climb a tree? Penelope decided to drop the subject. Arguing with Dill was like arguing with a cat.

They walked along for some time with Dill stopping every few moments. "You never can be too careful," he'd say and then peer under or around whatever happened to be in their path.

After a while, Penelope decided you *could* be too careful and never make it where you were going. "I think I'll go on ahead a bit," she said, pointing to the trees in the distance. "I'll wait for you there."

Dill stared ahead, his lips pursed. "Well . . ."

"I'll keep an eye out for wild boar, I promise."

"Oh, all right," he agreed.

Penelope ran down the path, relieved to finally be making some progress. She thought about the Shadow moving across the Realm and the Clockworkers swarming underneath it. Dill said they should head for the Range of Possibilities to escape them. But then what? Would that bring them any closer to finding the Great Moodler?

Penelope had hoped she could count on Dill to help her in the search, but now she wasn't so sure. He talked to flowers and thought wild boar were lurking in the bushes. Maybe he hadn't just lost his way — maybe he'd lost his mind as well!

She stopped running. *It's up to me*, Penelope realized. She wasn't used to things being up to her. Her mother usually made the plans and her father rubber-stamped them. That never left Penelope much to do. Until now. She suddenly had the urge to worry again. She couldn't help herself.

How will I ever find the Great Moodler . . .

All on my own . . .

With no help?

Penelope could feel her face growing warmer and warmer, but instead of the *pop-pop-pop* of worry warts, she heard a rustling noise.

Rustle. Rustle.

It was coming from the clump of bushes to her right.

It's probably just a squirrel, she told herself.

Rustle. Rustle. **Snap!**

Penelope froze, her eyes fixed on the spot where the sound had come from. Something was breaking branches. Something large. Penelope was about to run when she heard a series of muffled curses. Just then a man burst out, picking bits of twigs and leaves off his coat sleeves and grumbling loudly.

"Stupid, stupid leaves! What are they doing sticking to *me*? Don't they know who I am?"

Penelope let out a sigh of relief. The man didn't seem very friendly, but at least he wasn't a giant wild pig! He wore gray slacks, a gray shirt, and a gray tie. His skin had a soft gray pallor and his eyes were gray to match. Thin gray hair hung loosely around an angular face, marked by a pinched, unhappy mouth. When he caught sight of Penelope, however, a look of delight crossed his face and then immediately disappeared, as if he were expecting someone else.

"Hello," said Penelope hesitantly.

"Yes, yes, hello, it is." He continued brushing off his jacket, and then asked sharply, "Where are you going all alone, child?"

Penelope objected to being called a child, but was too polite to say so. "Oh, I'm not alone. I . . ."

The man stopped brushing. His eyes locked on Penelope. "Not alone? That's excellent!"

"Well, my friend and I . . ."

"Oh, yes, yes, 'your friend,' and who might that be?" He took an eager step forward.

"Dill and . . ."

"DILL!" shouted the man and rushed past Penelope, almost running over her in an attempt to get by.

Penelope looked back up the trail, and sure enough there was Dill on his hands and knees, looking under some bushes. In a flash the man was upon him. He grabbed Dill's arm and yanked him up. "So pleased to see you, Dill, really, really, it's wonderful. I can't *wait* to tell you what I've been up to."

"Uh . . . ur," stammered Dill. But it was too late. The man had already launched into his speech.

Penelope walked slowly up to the two men. The stranger was talking on and on, while Dill just stood there listening. "I had the most dreadful pain in my tooth," said the stranger. "My tooth hurt so much I woke up at 2:17

this morning. Or was it 2:18? No, it must have been 2:17, because I was in the kitchen for a glass of water by 2:18. Then I put some ice on my tooth, which didn't make a bit of difference. Not a bit, I can tell you."

And he did tell him. The man told Dill in the minutest detail everything about his toothache, rarely pausing for breath. Penelope thought that once he came to the end, he might stop. But he didn't. He just brought up another topic. And another. All the ailments he had ever suffered. All the trips to the post office he had ever taken. All the people who had ever irritated him.

Dill's eyes had a glazed and faraway look, while the strange man positively beamed. Penelope sighed loudly, hoping the man would take the hint. He ignored her. Penelope was used to being ignored, so she did what she always did in this situation. She made herself comfortable and waited. She sat on the ground, crossed her legs, and began to play her waiting games. First she played a game of throwing small rocks at an imaginary target. Then she leaned her head back and watched the clouds for interesting shapes. Next she looked for ants.

All the while, the man kept talking. His brilliant childhood, a book he was writing, tips on what to wear for every occasion. On and on and on. Penelope rested her head in her hands and closed her eyes. The man's voice became a drone in the background. She was just drifting off to sleep when — *plop! plop!* — something warm and wet hit the back of her neck.

Penelope jerked her head up. Dill was crying. Not really crying like he had hurt himself — crying like someone had turned on a faucet. His mouth and eyes were frozen in place while huge tears streamed down his cheeks.

Penelope jumped to her feet and gave Dill's arm a shake. It was stiff as a board. "Dill!" she shouted. "What's wrong?" No response. He'd lost the ability to speak, much less move.

The strange man didn't seem to notice. He was talking faster than ever, his mouth moving at an amazing speed. Everything about the man seemed more intense than before. Was his hair black now? And how about his clothes? They seemed more blue than gray.

"Excuse me." Penelope tried to interrupt. The man ignored her. He gripped Dill by the collar, pulled him in close, and began talking about his shopping habits.

"The proper way to shop is to start with the produce section. First you must check the tomatoes. I squeeze each one as hard as I can. I *only* eat firm tomatoes. Then you check the lettuce for bugs . . ."

Dill's tears dried up. The color drained from his face and was now leaving his neck. His bright red hair had faded to light pink. His eyes were like marbles, his body a statue.

Penelope grabbed the man's arm and shook it. "Will you *please* be quiet? Something is terribly wrong with my friend!"

"Hush!" snapped the man. "Don't bore me with your chatter."

"I'm not boring anyone. *You* are!" Before the words were out of her mouth, Penelope knew what was wrong. Dill had tried to warn her, but she hadn't understood. This man was a *Wild Bore*!

Dill wasn't stiff as a board. He was bored stiff! And the tears? Bored to tears. Soon he would be bored to death.

"Stop! Please stop!" Penelope pleaded with the Wild Bore. He never even blinked. His eyes were locked on Dill. Penelope didn't exist.

By now the Bore looked radiant. His once-gray hair was rich as midnight, and his gray eyes flashed every color in the rainbow — red, green, yellow, blue — a new color every few seconds. Dill, on the other hand, was white as chalk. Penelope grabbed his wrist, searching for a pulse. She couldn't feel anything!

Penelope was so desperate she flung herself at the Bore, kicking and screaming. "*Ayyyyyy!*"

The Bore fought back. "Run along, *child*. The grown-ups are busy!" His chatty, conversational tone was now a vicious snarl. He grabbed Penelope's arm and shoved her to the ground with a thud.

When Penelope fell, she landed on something stiff and lumpy. Her notebook! She sprang to her feet and snatched it from her pocket. Dill had said the only way to stop the Bore was to get a word in edgewise. That was exactly what she would do!

Penelope took out her pen and tore a piece of paper from her notebook. She would fight fire with fire. She would outwit the Wild Bore with words. But not just any words. Interesting words! The Bore might have shut her up, but she knew more than one way to be heard.

Penelope quickly wrote down the most interesting word she had ever seen. This was the bait. Then, on nine separate scraps of paper, she wrote nine more fascinating words. She didn't know what they all meant, but that didn't matter. In fact, that made them all the *more* fascinating. She stood on the tips of her toes and held up the most interesting word in the world for Dill to see:

Taj Mahal

"Stop that this instant!" squealed the Bore, pushing Penelope aside. But it was too late. Penelope had gotten a word in edgewise. Dill turned his head ever so slightly toward Penelope. Quick! She held up the next few words.

First Ambrosia, quickly followed by Nova.

That did the trick. A blush of color came into Dill's face and slowly he began to move his head away from the Bore and toward Penelope.

Penelope backed away, holding up one word and then the next:

Kumquat . . .

Cowpoke . . .

Conundrum . . .

Dill inched toward Penelope, his eyes locked on the tempting words. The Bore grabbed desperately at Dill, pleading, "Listen to me! Me! *Meeee!*"

Nebula, Doodle, Blurb.

The words were coming faster now and Dill walked with purpose after them. The color was rushing to his face and his red hair was ablaze! The Bore was almost out of earshot when Penelope silenced him with her final, fascinating word:

Skedaddle!

chapter ten

"That was a close call," said Penelope after the Wild Bore was safely behind them.

"Not at all!" countered Dill. He was walking briskly down the trail, swinging his arms and taking deep breaths. "As soon as I realized the Bore was ignoring you, I knew we'd be okay."

"You *did?*"

"Of course! You were a tremendous threat, but the Bore didn't seem to notice."

She was a tremendous threat? Penelope mulled this information over. It hardly seemed possible. She rarely had the upper hand in anything!

"From what I can tell," continued Dill, "the Wild Bore didn't think *you* were the least bit interesting, which means he didn't think you were very dangerous. You and I both know that's bunk. Rubbish. Total nonsense! Young people are the *most* interesting people around. But Wild Bores wouldn't know that. And do you know why?"

"No," said Penelope.

"Because they were never children! Of course, at one time they *looked* like children and could easily be *mistaken* for children, but they were really Little Knowitalls, which is a different thing altogether." Dill glanced over at her. "Certainly you've met a Little Knowitall?"

Penelope thought about the girl with pigtails from science camp. "Oh, yes," she said. "Lots of them."

"Well, then you know exactly what I'm talking about."

By now they had reached the row of trees where they were headed. Just as Dill had said, a creek wound its way through the tree roots. Dill found a shallow area scattered with rocks and leapt lightly from one to the next, chattering all the while. "Almost all Little Knowitalls become Wild Bores. Although now that I think about it, a few *do* manage to avoid that fate by learning to be inquisitive about something besides themselves." Dill reached the other side and turned back to look at Penelope. "Speaking of being inquisitive . . . how do you know all those fascinating words?"

"Oh, well, I don't know them *all*," Penelope explained, balancing her foot on a rock. "But I guess you can say I collect them." She raced across the creek and landed on the other side with a hop. "I never expected them to come in handy."

"Handy?" exclaimed Dill. "They were critical. Vital. Absolutely essential. I wouldn't have survived without them!"

Penelope beamed. She wasn't used to her words being important.

"I suggest you expand your collection immediately!" said Dill.

Penelope's smile faded. She thought about her notebooks filled with drawings and sketches, dreams and ideas. Ideas that would turn into stories if only she could get them flowing again. "I'm not sure there's any use," she mumbled.

Dill's eyes grew large. Huge, actually. For once, he didn't say anything. He just stared at Penelope, waiting for her to continue.

But she didn't *want* to continue. She didn't want to tell Dill the awful truth. It was no use collecting words because she would never use them. She would never be a writer, not if she couldn't moodle. Dill had said it himself — she was an anomaly. A failure.

Penelope stole a glance up at Dill. He was waiting patiently for her to speak. "I want to be a writer," she said, her voice still soft. "And I used to believe that one day I could be, even though my parents didn't think so. I was full of story ideas — so full I couldn't keep track of them all. But out of the blue they . . . they disappeared."

Dill took a step back.

"That's why I wanted to find the Great Moodler," Penelope rushed on. "I thought she could help me find out where all my ideas went, help me become a moodler again. If I can't moodle, I can't write."

"That," said Dill, pointing straight at her, "is a brilliant plan. You find the Great Moodler and get all your ideas back. And then the Great Moodler can find my lost way and I'll be an explorer again!"

This time it was Penelope's turn to take a step back. She hadn't expected Dill to actually *adopt* the plan. "But I've run out of ideas and can't moodle up any new ones. I'm not sure how to find her without . . ."

"You can do it," said Dill, cutting her off. "Look how you handled that Wild Bore!" He turned and began to climb up the creek bank. "You're young and inquisitive, a moodler and a word collector," he called out, listing her qualifications. "What more do you need?"

A lot! thought Penelope. Those traits hadn't led to much success in life so far. Besides, had Dill forgotten about her attempt to use the moodle hat? She had come up with nothing! Penelope was just about to remind Dill of this fact when he let out a sharp cry.

"It's gone!"

Penelope scrambled up the creek bank to join him. Standing atop it, she looked out on a vast plain of rocks and boulders. "What's gone?" she asked.

"The Range of Possibilities," wailed Dill, pointing off into the distance. "It used to be over there, along the horizon, and now it's gone!" He began to pace back and forth, wringing his hands. "You see what I mean? I can't find anything anymore, not even a mountain range. This is bad. Horrible. Completely horrendous!"

Penelope stared at the plain. It was empty of any scenery except for rocks. Miles and miles of rocks. It looked like it would be hard to cross. "What are we going to do now?" she asked.

"We'll just have to follow a hunch," said Dill. He stopped pacing and began to pat his pockets. "Do you have one? I seem to be all out."

"*Me?*" asked Penelope. "Why would I have a hunch? I have no idea where we are, much less where we should go."

"Hunches aren't ideas. They're inklings," explained Dill.

"Don't inklings just pop into your head?"

"Exactly. And they pop out just as quickly. That's why you've got to catch them when you can. Push everything out of your mind and see what pops out when you do. More than likely you'll see a hunch. That's when you snag it!"

"With your hands?"

Dill looked at her as if she'd just said the moon was made of cheese. "Of course not. By listening to it! But be sure not to think while you do it," he instructed. "Thoughts scare them away. Now then, clear your mind and then look around a bit. You look up, and I'll look down."

Penelope couldn't imagine what she was looking for, but she did as she was told. She cleared her mind and then followed Dill's lead. He was walking in circles with his hands clasped behind his back, looking at the ground. Penelope did the same, but looked up at the clouds.

Walking around and around, staring at the sky, made Penelope woozy. Being woozy kept her from thinking too much, which turned out to be a good thing. After walking for a few moments it dawned on her that she might feel less woozy if she stopped walking and focused on one specific spot. With her neck bent back, she locked her eyes on the spot above her nose. When her eyes focused, she saw the most unusual thing. There, on the tip of her nose, sat a small creature, so slight it seemed to be made of air.

Penelope froze, her eyes fixed on the tiny thing. "Dill!" she called in her very quietest whisper. "Dill, come here."

Dill rushed over. "Good job!" he said, slapping Penelope on the back.

Penelope stayed frozen in position. "Now what do I do?" she asked, hardly daring to move her mouth.

"Just relax and concentrate on the question: What do we do now?"

Penelope gently returned her head to an upright position. She crossed her eyes to check on the hunch. It was still there, resting on her nose.

"Hurry up," said Dill. "We don't want to wear the poor thing out."

Penelope looked around, searching for some sign or clue that would tell her what to do next.

"Don't try to figure it out," said Dill. "Just listen to your hunch."

"But I don't hear anything," said Penelope.

"You've got to *really* listen," urged Dill.

Penelope stopped looking around and relaxed. When she did, she heard a small voice coming from what sounded like inside her own head. "Look up," it said. Penelope immediately checked to see if the creature was still on her nose. It had disappeared. *Oh, well*, she thought, *here goes.*

She looked up.

There, along the far horizon, was a black speck moving quickly toward her. It grew larger every second. Dill noticed it, too, and stood still, watching it come closer. The speck was beginning to take shape. It looked like a bird — a *gigantic* bird — a bird the size of a small airplane.

"*RUUUN!*" Dill shouted and, clutching his head, darted this way and that, forward and back, dodging left, then right. Penelope didn't move. Something told her — was it a hunch? — she should stay right where she was. In seconds the bird was upon them. Dill froze in fear and then dove for cover behind a particularly large rock.

The bird circled around them a few times before touching down in a storm of dust. Once the air cleared, Penelope got a better look. It was a bright yellow bird with a long flourish for a tail. Black and gray bands striped its wings and an elaborate looping plume swayed on its forehead. Its beak was brilliant green and would have been beautiful if it didn't look so sharp.

"*Coo-Coo,*" called the bird.

Its voice was loud, but so lyrical that Penelope relaxed. *Something so lovely wouldn't eat a person*, she reassured herself.

The bird made a deep bowing motion, one wing outstretched and the other bent in toward its chest. "*Coo-Coo, Coo-Coo!*" This time it called out with more insistence.

"I think it's trying to tell us something," whispered Dill from behind the rock.

"I think you're right," agreed Penelope. "I'll try to talk back." Mustering her courage, she addressed the gigantic bird. "*Coo coo, coo coo,*" said Penelope in her best birdcall.

The bird cocked its head and half sang, half spoke, "How could . . . *you-you* . . . be *Coo-Coo?*"

"Oh, but I'm not," stammered Penelope. "I was just . . . I didn't expect . . . I mean . . ."

"And your friend?" said the bird, jumping onto the rock Dill was hiding behind and peering down at him with interest. "Is he *Coo-Coo . . . too-too?*"

"Certainly not!" said Dill, embarrassed at being caught hiding. He jumped to his feet and made a quick bow. "I'm Dill."

The bird looked him over. Up. Down. Left. Right. When he was done he turned back to Penelope.

"I'm Penelope," she said, introducing herself with a curtsy.

"I'm *Coo-Coo*," said the bird with a deep nod of his head.

"We're looking for the Range of Possibilities," explained Dill. "Do you know where it is?"

"I . . . *do-do*," sang the bird.

"But that's wonderful!" exclaimed Penelope. "Will you take us to it?"

The Coo-Coo made a slight fluttering motion with his wings. "*Coo-coo* . . . if you really want me . . . *to-to*." The giant bird crouched next to a large rock, and Penelope scrambled up and onto his back.

"I hate flying," groaned Dill. "It always upsets my stomach."

"It's the only way," said Penelope, coaxing him up.

When they both were settled, the Coo-Coo leapt into the air. Dill made a sound like a frightened cat and clutched Penelope's waist. Penelope, however, laughed with delight as the bird took off. She was reminded of her fantasy to travel the world by hot air balloon so she could see all the sights. This was much better!

They flew for miles while the rocky wasteland ran beneath them. Here and there boulders rose up, dotting the scenery with their jagged forms. Once, Penelope saw a herd of enormous honey-colored animals picking their way across the landscape. They looked like deer or antelope, but with much longer legs and strangely human faces. Their giant antlers were braided together like elaborate headdresses. When they saw the Coo-Coo, they stopped and bowed their heads in solemn greeting.

The bird called out, "*Coo-coo, coo-coo,*" and dipped his wings in salute.

"What *were* those?" Penelope had never seen such animals.

"Mountain Lopers. It's a . . . *true-true* . . . honor to see them. There are so very . . . *few-few* . . . left."

"Did you see them?" said Penelope with a quick glance back at Dill, but his eyes were clamped shut.

The image of the Mountain Lopers lingered in Penelope's mind — graceful, noble, and, somehow, sad. *Why were there only a few left? Where had they all gone?*

Just then a warm yellow cloud bank rolled across the sky to meet them. It quickly wrapped them in its soft color and the Mountain Lopers disappeared from view. Penelope relaxed her grip on the Coo-Coo's feathered neck and let her fingers trail beside her. She longed to touch the brilliant streaks of yellow and gold that billowed around them. The faster they flew, the richer the yellow grew. Soon the clouds were the color of egg yolk dotted with hints of pink and fuchsia.

When they burst through, a small chain of colorful mountains appeared below them. The range spanned from the deepest, darkest blue to the shiniest, brightest white and everything in between. The foot of each mountain was a single color — midnight blue, mossy green, burnt umber — and this color, whatever it was, was the darkest shade it could be. As the color moved up the mountain, the shade grew lighter and lighter until it reached the peak. The peaks were glorious pastels, shimmering with only the faintest pigment. There were about a dozen mountains surrounded like an island by the desert of rocks and rubble.

"Look!" cried Penelope and nudged Dill with her elbow. "It's the Range of Possibilities!"

Dill peeled one eye open and then, suddenly alert, the other. "But where are all the mountains?" he shouted against the wind.

"What do you mean? They're right *there*!" Penelope pointed at the peaks ahead.

"But how can that be? There used to be hundreds! Where did they all go?"

"*Coo-coo*," called the bird. "I'll show . . . *you-you*."

The little group of mountains huddled below them, but instead of landing, the Coo-Coo caught the wind and let it take them higher. Dill groaned in protest and closed his eyes again. Soon they were soaring over a brilliant blue peak on the northeastern edge of the range, heading straight for a dark cloud swirling above its summit.

As they drew closer, Penelope's heart began to beat faster. This wasn't a cloud. It couldn't be. No cloud was this dark — this thick. It covered the sky like a blanket, casting the translucent peak beneath it into a dull gloom. At that moment, she realized exactly where they were headed. They had come all this way to escape from the Shadow and now the Coo-Coo was taking them directly to it!

Penelope clutched the bird tightly as she felt a cold force emanating from the Shadow. She opened her mouth to warn Dill, and the cold slipped down her throat. "Dill . . ." Penelope gasped, before her voice gave out.

Dill leaned forward, daring a look over Penelope's shoulder, his face turning a slight shade of green. "Turn back!" he shouted at the bird.

But the Coo-Coo only flew faster, heading straight toward the Shadow until it enveloped them. A cold shock hit Penelope like icy water and she felt a painful pressure seize her upper body. The deeper into the Shadow the Coo-Coo flew, the greater the pressure became. It spread up her chest and into her throat, cutting off the air. Even though the great bird flapped his wings harder and faster, Penelope couldn't tell if he was moving or not. Everything inside the Shadow was so still. Penelope gripped the Coo-Coo's neck as a horrible thought crossed her mind.

Is he flying? Or falling?

Just when Penelope felt the blackness creep across her eyes, they burst

back into the day (or what passed for day under the Shadow). Penelope gasped for breath and let her eyes adjust to the dismal light. They had crossed over the peak. On the other side, the earth was barren, marked only by a strange black grid. There were no trees or greenery of any kind. Drifts of smoke climbed into the gray sky, filling the air with a horrible acrid smell. Penelope's eyes stung and her throat felt as if it had been turned inside out.

The Coo-Coo dropped lower. Penelope saw that the grid was a series of freshly tarred roads, crissing and crossing one another for miles. The farther the Coo-Coo flew, the more roads they saw. There were all kinds — highways, byways, toll roads, back roads, front roads — each very long and very straight. Giant trucks crawled like insects across them. Every scrap of earth not already paved was covered in digging, scooping, drilling machines.

Boom. Boom. Boom.

Waves of sound shook the air. The Coo-Coo veered back toward the mountain range in the direction of the sound, flapping his wings with renewed vigor. A massive pillar of smoke hovered at the foot of the mountain they had just flown over. They drew nearer to the smoke until they were almost engulfed in it, and then, as if on cue, the booming began again.

BOOM! BOOM! BOOM!

The Coo-Coo faltered in midflight. Penelope's stomach dropped to her toes, while Dill grasped her waist painfully. The bird regained his balance and flew on. By now they could see the pillar wasn't smoke at all. It was dust.

BOOM! BOOM! BOOM!

The mountain shuddered.

BOOM! BOOM! BOOM!

With a horrible crash, a massive chunk of indigo-colored rock tumbled to the earth. As it fell, the color faded until it hit the ground and broke into a million gray pieces. With each blast of dynamite, more and more of the mountain shattered. Great gashes appeared in its side and the peak wobbled dangerously until a final explosion sent it crashing down. The shimmering blue vanished in a pile of rubble.

When the dust settled, Penelope watched in horror as a swarm of bulldozers scooped up the rocks and dumped them into a great toothy machine.

CRUNCH. CRUNCH. CRUNCH.

The machine ground the rocks to bits and spat them out into a line of waiting dump trucks. Once a truck was full, it drove down a six-lane highway that stretched out of sight.

"I've seen enough!" cried Dill.

The Coo-Coo flapped his gigantic wings and up they went, into the Shadow waiting above.

chapter eleven

Penelope held her breath and closed her eyes, bracing herself for the sickening cold of the Shadow. When it hit, she tried to stay calm by counting down from one hundred.

99, 98, 97 . . .

Her teeth began to chatter . . .

86, 85, 84 . . .

Her hands grew numb . . .

63, 62, 61 . . .

Her head grew lighter and lighter until she forgot what number she was on.

55 . . . or was it 45?

And then, just when Penelope couldn't hold her breath any longer, the Coo-Coo burst out of the Shadow and into the clear evening sky. Penelope took a huge gulp of warm air and willed herself to forget the bitter chill.

The bird headed toward a plum-colored mountain directly below them. Very near its peak a house sat perched on top of two enormous boulders. The house looked like a Swiss chalet covered in elaborately carved figurines. A huge wooden bird sat with outstretched wings on top of a steep roof. Carved oak leaves curled upward on either side of the wooden bird and then cascaded down the house. More oak leaves formed a bed for a gigantic pair of wooden squirrels resting at the base.

Instead of a door, there was an opening with a platform directly under the pitched roof. Below the opening was the most striking feature of all: A clock face took up the entire front of the house.

"It's a cuckoo clock!" gasped Penelope.

Dill didn't even bother to look. "Are we there yet?" he whimpered.

The bird landed expertly on the platform and scurried toward the entrance. Once inside, he knelt so his guests could dismount. "*Coo-coo* . . . kick off your . . . *shoe-shoes*. Make yourself at home," he sang.

Penelope slid to the floor and looked around the room. Her gaze immediately settled on a giant bird's nest in the far corner. Instead of twigs, the Coo-Coo had fashioned his nest from logs. Tucked inside the logs were various odds and ends that spilled out of the nest and onto the floor — an old lawn chair, a bit of fencing, even the chrome handlebars of a bicycle.

The rest of the room was a mess. Every nook, every cranny, every corner was filled with stuff. Not just any stuff, though — *shiny* stuff. Bits of aluminum foil and old street signs papered the walls. A chandelier fashioned from hubcaps and hung with silverware lit the room. Old toys, glass bottles, and knickknacks sat on shelves strewn with silver tinsel.

Penelope found a metal folding chair and sat down, while Dill collapsed gratefully onto a bedraggled sofa. "This is terrible! Horrendous! Unbelievably bad!" He took out a handkerchief and began to wipe his forehead. "Chronos is expanding his reach in every direction. Now I know why the Shadow is over my meadow. Soon the entire Realm will be one big city!"

"But why do they have to tear down the mountains?" asked Penelope. They were so beautiful. So . . . so *extraordinary*. She couldn't believe anyone would want to destroy them.

"To make room for . . . *new-new* . . . buildings and roads," said the bird with a sigh. "These mountains used to be home to an entire flock of . . .

coo-coo . . . birds. But now there are only a . . . *few-few* . . . of us left." The bird shook his head, unable to continue, and his elaborate tail drooped.

Penelope remembered the Mountain Lopers making their way across the wasteland. No wonder they looked so sad. Their homes had been destroyed. She looked around the Coo-Coo's house. Soon it would be a pile of rubble, too.

Dill rested his head in his hands. "Chronos must be stopped," he wailed. "If only we could find the Great Moodler —"

At the sound of the Great Moodler's name, the Coo-Coo snapped to attention. "*COO-COO . . . COO-COO!*" he screeched, erupting into a series of *coo-coos* so loud, so vigorous, he nearly hit his head on the ceiling. Once he'd recovered, he scooped up Dill with his wings. "Only the Great Moodler can . . . *undo-do* . . . this destruction. She can moodle up a whole . . . *slew-slew* . . . of possibilities and restore the Range! I've been hoping someone would find her." The bird dropped his startled guest and stepped back, wings outstretched. "And now here . . . *you-you* . . . are!"

"I'm afraid you are mistaken," objected Dill, straightening his jacket. "I've already tried to find her and failed. Penelope is the one —"

The bird spun around and snatched up Penelope.

"Wait! You don't understand —" insisted Penelope, but her objections were muffled in the bird's feathers. Once the Coo-Coo finally let her go, she tried again to explain. "You don't understand. I can't find her either. I even tried the moodle hat and nothing happened. I have no idea where she is."

"But I . . . *do-do!*" sang out the bird and dashed over to a pile of junk in the corner. He began rummaging through it, tossing things over his shoulder as he did. Penelope ducked just in time to miss a metal trash can followed by its lid. She stood back up, only to drop to the floor again as bits of tin roofing and aluminum foil sailed past.

When the bird spun around, he was holding a shiny, glittering ball for Dill and Penelope to see. "It's a . . . *clue-clue,*" he said with great reverence.

Dill and Penelope leaned in for a better look. The ball was made of pure light. Etched on its surface were a series of words, each one glimmering faintly. The bird turned the ball this way and that so they could read what it said:

Look in the least likely place.

"What is it?" asked Penelope in a hushed voice.

"It's a possibility," answered Dill. He looked up at the bird in awe. "Wherever did you find it?"

The Coo-Coo inhaled a deep, shuddering breath that ruffled his feathers from the top of his head to the tip of his splendid tail. Exhaling, he settled them all back into place and then began his story.

"After the Great Moodler disappeared, I . . . *flew-flew* . . . over the Range of Possibilities every day, looking for a . . . *clue-clue* . . . to where she went.

And every day, my hopes of finding her . . . *grew-grew* . . . smaller and smaller until I gave up altogether. On that day a violent storm . . . *threw-threw* . . . me off course. The wind carried me higher than ever before and I saw, out of the . . . *blue-blue* . . . a shimmering mountain of white light. I was blinded for a moment. When I regained my sight, the mountain was gone from . . . *view-view* . . . and this was falling from the sky." The bird nodded at the possibility.

"'Look in the least likely place,'" said Dill, almost to himself.

"But where *is* the least likely place?" asked Penelope. She sank down into the couch, but sat right back up again. A thought had occurred to her: The least likely place the Great Moodler would go — and the last place in the world Penelope wanted to visit — was Chronos City!

No sooner had the thought come to mind, than — *woop* — the possibility began to grow.

"*Coo-coo!*" called out the bird in surprise.

Dill turned to look at Penelope. "Are you considering the possibility?" he asked.

Penelope nodded.

"And . . ."

Penelope cringed. "I think it might be Chronos City."

Wooop. The possibility grew even bigger.

Dill put his hand on Penelope's shoulder. "Looks like that's a real possibility," he said.

The bird began hopping from one foot to the other. "Please go look for her. Please, please! Chronos has decreed all . . . *Coo-Coo* . . . birds Impossible. We keep our own time, which is . . . *taboo-boo*. If I went into the City, a . . . *crew-crew* . . . of Clockworkers would snatch me up. But the . . . *two-two* . . . of . . . *you-you* . . . might have a chance." He gave Dill and Penelope a pleading look.

"But isn't it dangerous?" asked Penelope.

"I'm afraid it is," conceded Dill. "Chronos City is unsafe. Risky. Outright hazardous. But we can't stay here and we can't go home. We're surrounded by the Shadow. We have to try."

"*Yahoo-hoo . . . yahoo-hoo!*" hollered the bird. He began dancing around the room, knocking things off shelves and sending the chandelier shaking.

Penelope watched the Coo-Coo dance about. She didn't think there was much to celebrate. She and Dill were heading for the worst place in the world to find the one person who could help them. But Dill was no good at finding things anymore and Penelope was an anomaly, a failure. Still, even though the whole expedition seemed doomed, Dill was right. They had to try. Finding the Great Moodler wasn't just about getting Penelope's ideas flowing again. The homes — maybe even the lives — of Dill and the Coo-Coo and the poor Mountain Lopers depended on it.

At that moment, a chime began to ring. It was seven and the clock was marking the hour. "That's my . . . *cue-cue*," trilled the bird. He tucked the possibility away in a corner and rushed outside. Soon they heard him singing along with the chime. "*Coo-coo, coo-coo. Coo-coo, coo-coo . . .*"

Dill and Penelope walked over to the opening of the great clock and together they watched the bird sing the hour into existence. When he finished, the sun settled lower along the horizon and the noises of the day receded to a hum.

"I'll be back in a . . . *few-few* . . . minutes," called the Coo-Coo and leapt into the early evening sky. The bird dropped down through the high mountain air. Once he reached a lower altitude, he began to dart this way and that, his wide beak snapping.

"What's he doing?" Penelope asked.

"Catching Time Flies, I suppose," answered Dill. "I'm surprised there are any left considering Chronos has decreed fun Impossible." Dill glanced in Penelope's direction. "Time flies only when you're having fun, you know."

Penelope nodded. Oh, yes. She knew.

Dill stretched out his arm and swept it through the air as if to embrace the horizon. "The skies of the Realm used to be filled with Time Flies and Fancies, but now they're almost extinct."

"What are Fancies?" asked Penelope.

"Giant, fantastical creatures that whiz and bounce through the air. Used to be people were always taking off on Flights of Fancy and going on adventures," said Dill. "Chronos insisted Fancies were only figments of the imagination and soon everyone ignored them until they disappeared. Or starved to death. That reminds me . . ." Dill rummaged through his many pockets, pulling out one thing after another — a ball of string, three pairs of glasses, an assortment of screws. Suddenly a smile spread across his face. "Ah, yes! Here they are." He whipped out two small brown-paper packages and held them out to Penelope. "Mushroom butter or mushroom loaf?"

Penelope pointed to the one on the right. "I'll take that one."

"Mushroom butter it is! Wise choice."

Penelope peeled back the wrapping on her sandwich. A nondescript gray substance was spread in a thick layer between two slices of bread. She took a small, uncertain bite and was surprised to find it tasted a little bit like peanut butter and a whole lot like chocolate.

"What did I tell you?" said Dill through a mouthful of sandwich. "Wise choice."

After the first bite, Penelope hardly tasted her sandwich. She was too busy thinking about the journey ahead. "Are you sure we should go to Chronos City?" she prodded Dill.

"I can't think of a more unlikely place to find the Great Moodler," he answered. "Can you?"

"No, but won't there be Clockworkers on the lookout? What if we get caught and taken to the tower?"

Dill stuffed the last bit of sandwich into his mouth and began to lick his fingers clean. "I agree," he said in between licks. "That *is* a possibility."

Penelope put down her sandwich. She wasn't hungry anymore. "And where will we look?"

"No idea," said Dill. "You could try the moodle hat again. I brought it along."

Penelope shook her head. Nothing came to mind before. It was bound to happen again. "I guess we'll just have to hope for some awfully good hunches," she said.

Dill nodded. "A hunch can take you a very long way."

The Coo-Coo returned from his dinner and the rest of the evening was spent planning their search for the Great Moodler.

First thing in the morning, the bird would take Dill and Penelope to the farthest reaches of Chronos City. If he came any closer, he risked being seen and taken away. The Coo-Coo would return to the same spot in three days to see what they had discovered. At that point they would regroup and decide what to do next. Nobody talked about what they would do if Dill and Penelope didn't discover anything, or if they got captured by Clockworkers. It was too terrifying.

Once the plan was settled, they all went to bed. Dill and Penelope slept on the floor on pallets stuffed with the Coo-Coo's giant feathers. The Coo-Coo slept in his nest, head tucked under a wing, his plume bobbing in time to his snores. Every sixty minutes he popped awake and scurried outside to sing the hour. None of this seemed to disturb Dill, but Penelope always woke with a start. At first she used the time to write in her notebook, capturing with words as best she could the events of her day. But soon she grew too tired to hold her pen, so she simply lay awake trying to imagine what her parents were doing. Were they trying to find her? Was her mother organizing a search party? Was her father giving pep talks to worried parents in the neighborhood? Or had they simply gotten on with their lives as if she had never existed? When sleep finally overtook her, Penelope fell into a dream.

She was riding on the Coo-Coo's back, soaring over the Range of Possibilities. Her mother was seated behind her, smiling and laughing, pointing at the beautiful mountains. It was wonderful! Penelope flung open her arms and trailed her fingers in the air. *Splat!* Something soft and sticky stuck to her hands. It smelled like daisies. She licked her fingers. Clouds! She was eating fluffy white clouds and they tasted like cotton candy, just as she always thought they would. Penelope reached out for more, but instead of sticking to her fingers, the clouds shrank back. Penelope looked over her shoulder. The Shadow was rolling across the sky, consuming everything in its path. The clouds were disappearing as if sucked up into a vacuum.

The Coo-Coo sensed the danger and began to struggle, beating his wings harder and faster. "Hold on!" shouted Penelope to her mother. Her mother dug her nails into Penelope's waist, but the pull of the Shadow was too strong. Her grip weakened. "Don't let go!" Penelope pleaded, but it was too late.

Whoosh!

There was a horrible sucking sound and her mother vanished into the darkness.

Penelope longed to cry out, to tell her mother she would save her, but she could hardly breathe, much less speak. She felt like a rock, heavy and dumb. A thousand pounds at least. The Shadow drew closer, stretching out to meet her. Soon it would swallow her.

Penelope felt herself sliding off the bird and everything faded into black.

chapter twelve

"Wake up! Wake up!"

Penelope opened one frazzled eye. Dill was leaning over her, pack in hand. "Come *on*!" he begged.

She struggled to sit up. "What's wrong?"

The Coo-Coo stood near the doorway, hopping nervously about. "*Coo-coo!* Time we . . . *flew-flew!*"

"Yes, yes, yes! We've got to go!" Dill practically screamed. "No time for explanations."

Penelope stumbled over to the Coo-Coo, slipping on her shoes as she went. Dill cupped his hands together to make a step and Penelope climbed onboard the bird's back. Once she was settled, Dill took a running leap and landed — *umph* — behind her. He was barely able to fling his legs up and over before the agitated bird bolted out the door and into the dawn.

Penelope couldn't understand what was wrong. It was a beautiful morning. The arms of the sun were just beginning to stretch across the sky. Where the sunlight touched, white clouds turned gold. The gold was reflected in the mountaintops and made their pastel peaks shine. Below the peaks, birds were waking the world with the first songs of day.

"Why are we in such a hurry?" she shouted.

Almost as if in answer she heard the boom of dynamite. Penelope looked down. Swarms of trucks were at the foot of the Coo-Coo's mountain.

"A . . . *crew-crew* . . . of workers arrived at my mountain first thing this morning," called the bird.

"They've picked up their pace!" yelled Dill. "We've got to hurry."

The bird veered sharply to the east toward Chronos City — toward the Shadow. Even though morning had arrived over the Coo-Coo's mountain, the air here had a gray pallor, as if the sun were shining through a dirty filter. Penelope stared at the wasteland below them. Now she knew the miles of rocks and boulders were the remains of once-beautiful mountains. The farther they flew, the flatter the terrain below them grew. The rocks and boulders turned to pebbles and dust. The pebbles and dust turned into a dirt road, and the dirt road gave way to asphalt. The City had begun.

The bird started a slow, circling descent before landing near a large rock. Dill and Penelope quickly dismounted. When they were both safely on the ground, Dill turned to the Coo-Coo, hand outstretched. "We'll do our best to find the Great Moodler," he promised. "Thank you for all your help."

"Yes," agreed Penelope, holding her hand out as well. "Thank you."

The Coo-Coo hesitated for a moment before rushing at Dill and Penelope and scooping them up in his wings. Huge tears slid down his face and splashed onto the asphalt. "*Boo-hoo-hoo* . . . *boo-hoo-hoo*," he cried. "Please . . . *do-do* . . . be careful."

Dill and Penelope made repeated, although muffled, promises to be as careful as they could and return to this spot in three days with any news of the Great Moodler. The Coo-Coo finally released them and took off into the air. Dill and Penelope watched him until he disappeared, and then they turned to face the road.

"Here goes," said Dill, his voice grim.

Penelope shuddered. "Here goes."

Off they went, heading for the City, their hearts heavy with the memory of the Clockworkers waiting at the foot of the Coo-Coo's mountain.

As they walked, the sun rose higher in the sky and the day grew warm. After a while, the road widened from a single lane to two, then three, before blossoming into an intersection. The intersection was shaped like the spoke of a wheel, with roads stretching in twelve different directions. Off in the distance they could see the outline of the City, running across the entire horizon like a wall.

Dill and Penelope came to a halt. "Which road should we take?" asked Penelope. There were so many to choose from. How would they know which one was right?

Just then Dill's stomach let out a loud growl. "I'd say follow a hunch, but I'm so hungry I doubt I could get very far. Let's eat breakfast." Dill dug around in his pack for a moment before unearthing a small brown envelope. "Hold out your hand," he instructed, and shook a bunch of tiny gray pellets into Penelope's palm. Penelope just assumed they were some sort of mushroom and popped them into her mouth.

"Good gracious," cried Dill. "One at a time!"

Too late. The tiny pellets exploded in Penelope's mouth, filling it with a sticky, puffy substance. The pellets grew to five times their original size. Then ten times. Then twenty.

"You're eating mushmellows," explained Dill. "A cross between mush-rooms and marshmallows. I invented them as rations for long trips. But you really *should* eat them one at a time."

Penelope tried to say, "Got it." But it came out more like "*Awt ehh.*"

"You could live off these for days and days," Dill rattled on, popping a mushmellow in his own mouth. "They're full of protein and all sorts of nutri-ents. Not to mention, they're yummy. Delicious. Absolutely scrumptious."

Penelope just nodded. Her cheeks were so full they were beginning to hurt. She tried to move the mushmellows around in her mouth, but there was no room to maneuver.

"Try sucking on it," offered Dill and delicately placed another pellet on his tongue.

Penelope squeezed in her cheeks and tried to draw a breath. *Gurgle.* An odd sound came from the back of her throat as her saliva went to work breaking down the sticky substance. After a few moments the mushmellows began to shrink and slid down her throat.

Gurgle. Gurgle. This time the gurgling sound came from her stomach. Penelope looked down in surprise. The mushmellows had continued to expand. It looked like she was carrying a bowl underneath her overalls.

"Just a minor side effect," said Dill, patting his own protruding belly. "It'll go down in a minute. I might need to fiddle with the recipe a bit." They sat there quietly, digesting their breakfast, until Dill let out a laugh. "Look! I've got a hunch!" He was staring out of the corner of his eye at a tiny, translucent creature on his shoulder. He cocked his head to one side so he could listen to it better. "Someone's coming," he said slowly, as if repeating what he heard.

Penelope didn't like the sound of that. She quickly swallowed the last of her mushmellows. "Someone *who?*" she asked.

Dill listened to his hunch, his thick brows huddled over his eyes. "Someone . . . someone . . . from the City," he said finally.

They heard them before they saw them. Far off in the distance came the sound of sirens. The sound grew louder and louder as it grew closer and closer. Soon they saw the lights — flashing lights that quickly became police cars. The cars approached from every direction, speeding down each of the twelve roads until . . .

Screech. Twelve squad cars came to a stop at the same exact moment.

Click. Twelve car doors opened and twelve uniformed police officers stepped out.

Slam. Twelve car doors closed.

Twelve police officers glared from under twelve hats, their lips flattened in grim frowns. Each officer had a large patch sewn onto his or her left shoulder with black, angular markings on it: I, II, III, IV, V . . . Penelope knew what the markings were — she had seen them before on a grandfather clock. VI, VII, VIII . . . They were Roman numerals and they were used to mark time. IX, X, XI . . . Sure enough, the numbers went all the way to: XII.

Suddenly a voice shouted at them through a bullhorn.

"HALT RIGHT THERE!"

Dill and Penelope stood frozen in the middle of the intersection as a peculiarly short police officer stepped forward. He was shaped like a fire hydrant, with a square lump of a head sitting on a pair of neckless shoulders. "It's 10:00 a.m. and you're under arrest for idling at the crossroads. I am Officer X, man of the hour and keeper of the timepiece." The policeman whipped out a pocket watch and dangled it in front of Penelope and Dill. "As you can see, you've disturbed the piece."

The watch did seem disturbed. The second hand swung wildly around and the minute hand was actually moving backward. Officer X snatched the watch back and snapped the cover closed. "You'll have to come with me," he barked.

Penelope's mouth dropped open. They *couldn't* go with him. This wasn't part of the plan! She whirled around and stared at Dill, willing him to do something.

Dill straightened his jacket and then cleared his throat. "Excuse me, sir, but we —"

"*Now!*" yelled the officer, pointing at the squad car. "We haven't got all day."

Dill and Penelope both cringed and scurried over to the car. Once they reached the door, Officer X leaned forward and snatched Dill's pack from his back. "I'll take that," he said, dumping the contents on the ground. He poked at things with his foot, making sure to stomp on the leftover sandwiches. He stopped when he saw the moodle hat. "What's this?"

Penelope held her breath. What would Dill say? If moodling was illegal, then having a moodle hat was certainly forbidden. Dill just shrugged an innocent shrug. "A toy," he answered.

In its collapsed state, the hat did look like it could be a toy. Officer X must have thought so, too, because he picked it up and threw it as far as it would go. Then he turned back to Dill and Penelope and opened the car door. "Get in."

They did as they were told. Officer X slammed the door and slid behind the wheel. He executed a quick U-turn and sped off in the direction he had come. Eleven police cars followed, sirens screaming.

-- -- --

As they drove, the monstrous skyline of Chronos City came closer and closer. Buildings crowded the sky like giants fighting for air, their heads lost in the Shadow, their feet swarming with cars. The outskirts of the never-ending City were full of bulldozers, concrete mixers, and giant cranes. It seemed like a new building was completed every minute and caravans of moving trucks clogged the highways.

Penelope thought about the Coo-Coo. They were tearing down his mountains for *this*? It was too horrible to think about! And now their plan to help — to find the Great Moodler and stop Chronos — was ruined. Penelope would never moodle again . . . Dill would never find his lost way . . . and the Coo-Coo's home would be destroyed. Penelope felt more like an anomaly than ever!

Just then Dill reached over and gave her hand a squeeze. "Don't worry," he whispered and began poking his face all over as if counting warts.

Penelope smiled weakly. He was right. Now was not the time to worry. It wouldn't help a bit. Instead, she needed to focus and start working on a new plan. She took a deep breath and tapped her forehead. Dill gave her a knowing look and tapped his forehead, too. Good. They were both working on it. Together they would figure out something.

Penelope peered out of the squad car, trying to determine where they were. The city was built around one gigantic structure — the clock tower. It was taller than the tallest skyscraper and visible from every corner of the City. Its sharp spire pointed imperiously at the sky. Beneath the spire were four clock faces, one on each of its four sides. The clock faces shone with a garish green light. They peered down on the City, bathing it in a hateful glow. The sun was nowhere to be seen.

Even from miles away, Penelope could see exactly what time it was on the tower: 10:48 and 32 seconds . . . 33 seconds . . . 34 seconds . . . She was mesmerized by the second hand as it swung around and around. *Where did all the time go?* she wondered.

Dill nudged her sharply. "If you stare at it too long, you'll reset your internal clock."

Penelope looked away from the clock and watched the scenery instead. By now the highway had turned into a twenty-lane expressway. All the cars they passed were either black or white, depending on their size. Officer X merged into a special lane reserved for police, and soon they were moving at high speed, leaving the traffic behind in a blur. Penelope read the billboards whizzing past.

IDLENESS IS THE GREATEST PRODIGALITY.

LOST TIME IS NEVER FOUND AGAIN.

ALL THINGS ARE EASY TO INDUSTRY,
ALL THINGS DIFFICULT TO SLOTH.

Oh, shut up, thought Penelope. There was something irritatingly familiar about these sayings. She glanced back up at the clock tower. *Just to check the time,* she told herself. Penelope could only see one clock face, but it seemed to be staring right at her. The second hand . . .

22 . . . 23 . . . 24 . . .

moved beautifully around . . .

25 . . . 26 . . . 27 . . .

and around.

Penelope scrunched her eyes and gave her head a quick shake. She leaned back in the seat and tried to erase the image of the clock tower from her mind.

Dill had said staring at the tower would reset her internal clock. But what exactly was an internal clock? She remembered a painting she had seen in a book. There was a clock that looked like it was made of Silly Putty. It hung draped over a tree limb, almost ready to slide off onto the ground. *Is that what my internal clock looks like?* she wondered. Penelope didn't think so. Her clock had wings, she decided. Instead of a nasty beeping alarm, it tickled her when it was time to go somewhere.

Just then Dill put his hand on her shoulder. "We're *here*," he whispered. Something about the way he said "here" made Penelope's throat constrict. Before she could take a good look out the window, the car came to an abrupt halt and Officer X hopped out. "Let's go!" he snapped.

Dill and Penelope stepped out of the car and into a dark terminal. The terminal had a low concrete ceiling and concrete walls to match. On each wall a large metal clock chipped away the time, filling the air with its ticking. Everywhere Penelope looked, she saw men and women in identical blue coveralls and hats moving stiffly in and out of dark gray doors.

"Where are we?" she asked.

Officer X turned to look at her, a menacing glare in his eyes. "We're in the clock tower, young lady. It's time for *you* to get busy."

chapter thirteen

Officer X escorted Dill and Penelope to a counter at the far end of the terminal. A few people stopped to stare at them and Dill smiled and nodded politely. "For goodness' sake, stop that!" scolded Officer X. "This isn't a parade." He tried to glare up at Dill, but he was too short. He ended up glaring at Dill's belt buckle, which didn't do much to improve his mood.

At the counter, Officer X was officially assigned to Dill and Penelope's case and given a stack of forms to fill out. After each one was properly signed, stamped, and filed, Officer X turned and pointed to a set of double doors to their right. "March!"

Penelope didn't feel the least bit like marching, but she followed Dill's lead and marched all the same.

Dill's legs were so long he reached the doors first. "Stop!" Officer X screamed at him and ran to catch up. He arrived with a red face and his shirt untucked. "Forget marching." He rearranged his uniform and badge and then pushed past Dill. He brought out a large set of keys, found the right one, and the doors opened with a groan.

Inside was a long, dimly lit hallway filled with doors. Each door was exactly like the others except for the sign posted above it. "Crime Units!" declared Officer X, pointing at the signs. "Dawdling, Dillydallying, Feet Dragging, Frittering, Lollygagging, and Puttering. Never forget," he said, fixing them both with a stare, "the Clockworkers of the Realm are everywhere, protecting the populace against the evils of time wasters."

One of the doors swung open and Penelope caught a glimpse inside. Rows and rows of desks filled a long room. Men and women dressed in identical blue coveralls sat upright at the desks. They looked exactly like the people Penelope had seen in the terminal. They were all typing in unison. *Click-clack. Click-clack. Click-clack.* They struck each key at precisely the same time. *How did they do that?* Penelope wondered, before the door closed and the scene vanished.

At the end of the hall, another set of double doors waited for them. As they approached, the doors slid open with a *hiss* to reveal a cavernous courtroom. Low fixtures dropped yellow pools of light on a massive podium at the far end of the room. Two figures sat expectantly at the podium. Their nameplates read JUDGE JUST RIGHT and JUDGE JUST SO. An enormous 60-second stopwatch hung on the wall behind the judges. Under the stopwatch a sign declared: JUSTICE IN UNDER A MINUTE.

The judges perked up at the sight of the new arrivals. "Don't just stand there, we don't have all day," screeched Judge Just So.

"Time's a-wasting," shrieked Judge Just Right, motioning Dill and Penelope to approach.

Once they were standing in front of the judges, Dill spoke up. "Your Honors . . ."

"Silence," barked Judge Just So and slammed her gavel on the podium. *Bam!*

"Silence," repeated Judge Just Right and slammed *her* gavel. *Bam!*

"*I* said, Silence!" *Bam! Bam!*

"*I* said, SILENCE!" *Bam! Bam! Bam!*

The two judges shouted and banged until both of their faces were red. This might have gone on all day if Officer X hadn't cleared his throat with a cough.

The banging stopped. The gavels hung in the air.

"Well," said Judge Just Right, "speak up."

Officer X stepped forward, his chest outthrust. "These two citizens were caught idling at an intersection on the outskirts of Chronos City."

Judge Just Right fixed Dill with a stare. "And what do you have to say for yourself?"

"Your Honors," Dill said again, this time with a deep bow, "we were simply eating breakfast when —"

"Likely story!" screamed Judge Just Right. *Bam!* went the gavel. "As for *you*, young lady," she said, pointing at Penelope, "what were you doing idling at an intersection?"

Before Penelope could say a word, Judge Just So picked up a large black book from a shelf below her podium. She adjusted her glasses and read solemnly, "Be always ashamed to catch thyself idle."

Judge Just Right snatched her own book out. "Trouble springs from idleness . . ."

"The busy man has few idle visitors," interrupted Judge Just So.

"TO THE BOILING POT THE FLIES COME NOT!"

Penelope groaned. She had the feeling she had heard all this before.

The judges stopped their squalling and looked at her expectantly.

"Go on," demanded Judge Just So. "Tell us what you were doing."

Penelope knew better than to mention their search for the Great Moodler. Before she could think of the right thing to say, she heard herself answer, "Nothing."

"*GUILTY!*" both judges shouted, leaping from their seats and frantically fighting to start the stopwatch.

Judge Just So hit the button first and began the sentencing. "For idling at an intersection . . ."

Tick, tick, tick . . .

"And for doing *ab-so-lutely* nothing," snarled Judge Just Right.

Tick, tick, tick . . .

"You are hereby sentenced to twenty minutes . . ."

Tick, tick, tick . . .

"Around the clock."

Brriiing! The sound of the stopwatch filled the room.

"Take them away!"

-- -- --

That wasn't so bad, thought Penelope as Officer X ushered them out of the courtroom and into a waiting elevator. They were only sentenced to twenty minutes around the clock. She wasn't sure what that meant, but she knew she could put up with almost anything for twenty minutes.

Once inside the elevator, the doors slid shut and the compartment rushed soundlessly upward. Penelope watched through a small window as the great City flashed by. The higher they went, the smaller the City became, until the buildings looked like toy blocks.

They stood looking out on a room at the very top of the tower. Four impossibly E-NOR-MOUS clocks made up its walls. Gigantic hands marched around clock faces that were — eight, nine, ten? — stories high. The vibration of their thunderous ticking shook the air. The clocks glowed a greenish-yellow that robbed everything of its natural color. Blues looked gray. Reds looked brown. And skin tones? They were the worst. Dill and Officer X were both a strange and unhappy olive green.

Through the thick, clear glass of the clocks, Penelope could see the sky, or what she assumed was the sky. The Shadow hung like a blanket over the tower and turned the day a dull gray infused with the tower's unnatural fluorescent light.

An engine made of a million moving parts sat in the middle of the room. Knobs and dials, rods and levers, blinking, beeping consoles — all of them worked to power the great clocks. Whirring, grinding gears churned around and around, endlessly feeding into one another. Gears spun, springs sprang, pistons pumped, and gray-blue smoke rings rose from exhaust pipes.

A swarm of workers dressed in blue coveralls and blue hats tended to all the equipment. They looked exactly like the people Penelope had seen in the terminal and offices outside the courtroom. She realized they must be Clockworkers. They moved with a regimented precision dictated by the beat of the four clocks. *Tick*. A hand went up. *Tock*. A knob was pulled. *Tick*. The knob was released. *Tock.* The hand went down. Several Clockworkers with silver badges on their chests stood on a high platform rhythmically scanning the room.

Just then, the clocks began to chime eight o'clock. *GONG, GONG, GONG . . .* The sound made Penelope's knees shake and her teeth chatter. Dill had the good sense to stick his fingers in his ears, and Penelope quickly followed suit.

When the gonging stopped, Officer X took out his pocket watch. "Right on time," he said smugly. "Which means, you two had better get to work. As you can see, you'll be working around the clock for the duration of your sentence."

Oh, yes, Penelope could see. Now she knew *exactly* what working around the clock meant.

Officer X slapped Dill and Penelope both on the back (a little harder than Penelope thought necessary) and disappeared down the stairs.

One of the Clockworkers approached. She greeted Dill and Penelope with a stiff bow. "You-are-quite-wel-come-to-the-clock-tow-er," she said, each word uttered in time with the ticking clock.

"Oh, hello," said Dill, bowing back.

"Ver-y-well-thank-you." The Clockworker bowed again. There was some-thing off about her response and her excellent manners, as if she were reading them from a script.

The Clockworker turned to Penelope and repeated her greeting, then

chapter fifteen

"You've woken them," whispered the Timekeeper.

Penelope peeled her hand away from her mouth. "Woken what?" she managed to say.

"The Fancies. This prison is full of them."

"*What?*" asked Dill in surprise. "You mean those dust bunnies sleeping in the cells are Fancies?"

"Indeed," said the Timekeeper. He got up from his chair and shuffled to the cell door, careful not to trip over his trailing beard. The Fancies had somehow managed to escape their cells and were crowding the halls, chattering loudly. The Timekeeper reached through the bars and began to pet the tiny creatures.

"How can these be Fancies?" said Dill, joining the Timekeeper at the door. "The Fancies I remember were glorious. Magnificent. Astonishingly beautiful."

"If they're so wonderful," said Penelope, "why are there warning signs everywhere? Are they dangerous?"

"Some would say they're dangerous," answered the Timekeeper. "They certainly are powerful, but only if they're fed. Which of course they're not. Or at least not anymore. That's why they're so thin and drab."

"What *exactly* do they eat?" asked Penelope. She wanted to know just how dangerous these little creatures were.

"Tickles," said Dill.

"Tickles?" Penelope let out a nervous laugh. When she did, the Fancies began, for just the briefest moment, to glow.

"That's the spirit!" said the Timekeeper.

The Fancies hummed and twittered with pleasure.

"It used to be everyone had their very own Fancy. People tickled them quite regularly and rode them on great adventures. Just like Dill said, they were beautiful — huge and fluffy with wild colors and even wilder antics. But feeding the Fancies was declared Impossible long ago and so they withered away to almost nothing. It wasn't long before they were rounded up and imprisoned as a public nuisance. Now all they do is sleep. I'm sure they haven't been fed for . . ." The Timekeeper searched for the exact time and finally decided on "eons."

Penelope got up and cautiously approached the bars. All the eyes turned in her direction. "How did they get out of their cells?" she asked.

"Oh, my, no cell can keep the Fancies from being free," replied the Timekeeper. "They stay inside the tower because they're simply too weak to go anywhere else. It would take something extraordinary — something truly Impossible — to fatten them up enough to fly away. But that will never happen. Chronos has seen to that."

At the sound of Chronos's name, there was a rushing sound like a thousand birds taking flight, and the Fancies scattered back to their cells. "Ah, well, there they go," said the Timekeeper. He turned toward the table, and Dill helped him to his seat.

"The sound of the Great Moodler's name must have woken them," said the Timekeeper. "I'm sure they miss her terribly. As do I."

"You *do*?" said Dill, nearly dropping the Timekeeper into his chair.

"Of course I do! Oh, I suppose that's Impossible, too," he said with a wave of his hand, "but ever since I lost track of time, I haven't cared a whit for Chronos's decrees. The Great Moodler moodled up the most beautiful possibilities. What's the harm in that?"

Dill and Penelope both sat down and leaned over the table toward the Timekeeper. "Tell me," said Penelope, "do you happen to know where the Great Moodler might be?"

The Timekeeper let out an enormous yawn and then answered, "Certainly!"

"*Where?!*" Dill and Penelope shouted at once.

But the Timekeeper was already asleep, his chin resting on his chest, his head swaying slightly with each breath.

Dill cleared his throat loudly, and the Timekeeper started awake. "Is it time to eat yet?"

"Not yet," said Dill.

"This is bad. Rotten. No good," said Dill, wringing his hands. "We *almost* had him."

Penelope wasn't listening. She took a deep breath and then shouted at the top of her lungs, *"WAKE UP!!"*

The Timekeeper jolted awake.

"Once we're under the clock, what do we do?" Penelope begged, clutching his arm.

For a brief moment he looked at her, eyes wide. "Hold on a second . . ." he mumbled.

So Penelope did. She sat and waited for him, listening for his final words. But they never came. The Timekeeper collapsed onto the table and was immediately engulfed in a tide of sleep, and no amount of shaking would wake him.

-- -- --

Dill and Penelope stayed up late discussing what they'd learned from the Timekeeper. They both agreed they couldn't work around the clock another day. The constant ticking was so overwhelming that if they didn't do something immediately, they would turn into Clockworkers and never find the Great Moodler or see the Coo-Coo ever again! If the Timekeeper didn't wake up and finish giving them instructions by the time Officer X returned, they would have to go on without him. The risk of waiting was too great.

Penelope offered to be the one to find the door. The Timekeeper had said the door was tiny, and that meant Penelope was the one more likely to see it. In the meantime, Dill would create a diversion to keep the Clockworkers from interfering in the search. Once Penelope found the door, they would go through it and position themselves outside the tower under the north clock. There they would figure out how to bring about the no-time. From what the Timekeeper had said, once they caused a no-time they would be outside the Realm of Possibility entirely. That's where they'd find the Great Moodler.

How she fell asleep that night, Penelope never knew. She must have, though, because morning came and a new day began just like the one before.

The intercom announced it was time to get up, breakfast was served, and, as usual, the Timekeeper slept through it all. Both Dill and Penelope tried to rouse him. They waved toast in front of his nose, pulled his beard, and dropped silverware next to his ears. They were both singing as loudly as they could and marching around the table when Officer X came to collect them.

"Hop to it!" Officer X shouted, rattling the cell door and bringing them to attention.

They obediently filed out of the cell and down the corridor. When Officer X wasn't looking, Penelope stole quick peeks at the Fancies. There they were — small, drab, gray creatures, all sound asleep. Did they *really* rush out of their cells last night? It hardly seemed possible.

They exited the prison and once again made their way down the empty hall toward the alcove. Dill took long, quick steps, and Penelope had to practically jog to keep up, but she didn't mind. Watching Officer X scurry after him, red-faced and scowling, was enough to lift her spirits. This little distraction didn't last long, however. Soon they were through the round door, up the stairs, and waiting at the threshold of the clock room.

"In you go," said Officer X, shoving them inside, clearly glad to be rid of them.

The Clockworker who was waiting to receive them bowed with typical exaggerated politeness. Penelope couldn't tell whether it was the same one as the day before. They all looked disturbingly similar. While the Clockworker escorted them to their stations, Penelope tried to look for the tiny door. But the Clockworker kept politely redirecting her steps.

Once they took their places at the conveyor belt, Penelope felt the tug of the familiar rhythm. *Tick-tock-tick-tock.* In a matter of moments, the ticking of the clock felt like the beat of her own heart. She knew it wouldn't be long before it took over completely. They would have to act soon if they were going to act at all.

Penelope looked up from her work to catch Dill's eye. To her surprise, he was standing idly by, fiddling with his ears. The Clockworkers on either side of him were still moving at their steady rhythm, sorting tokens. But without Dill's help, they couldn't keep up. Soon the conveyor belt was strewn with loose time.

Two of the Clockworkers with silver badges climbed down from their platform and walked deliberately toward Dill. "Back-to-work-if-you-please," they repeated over and over as they drew near.

Dill paid them no mind. He picked up a time piece, looked it over, and bit it gently. He made a nasty face and picked up a second token. He held a token in each hand, palms up. He moved his hands up and down, as if comparing their weight.

The Clockworkers were almost upon him, and Penelope knew her time had come. Dill looked right at her and gave her a wink. Then, much to her surprise, he grabbed a whole handful of tokens and stuffed them into his suit pockets.

The two official-looking Clockworkers rushed at Dill. "Stop-right-now! Steal-ing-time-is-for-bid-den." At that moment, a gigantic alarm clock began to ring furiously. It was louder than a freight train and accompanied by all sorts of flashing lights and warning bells.

The Clockworkers didn't seem to know what to do when something out of the ordinary happened. They stood frozen at their stations while the siren wailed.

This was the diversion Penelope was waiting for! She dropped down on all fours and crawled under the conveyor belt. Once she was out of the way of all the commotion, she popped out the other side and ran. She didn't know which was the north clock, so she decided to run around the perimeter of the room until she found the door. Suddenly a Clockworker stepped out from behind a tangle of thick wires connected to the time machine. "If-you-will-excuse-me," he said, moving in front of Penelope and blocking her path. He held a very large wrench in one hand and an oilcan in the other.

Penelope's mind raced. *Use your head!* she told herself. *Fight fire with fire!* What fire did the Clockworkers have besides their stiff, unrelenting politeness?

Well, decided Penelope, *I can be polite, too.* She turned toward the Clockworker and smiled sweetly. "May I please borrow your wrench?" she asked.

"But-of-course." The Clockworker held it out.

"Thank you so much." Once Penelope had the wrench firmly in her grasp she threw it as hard as she could into the heaving mass of gears running the time machine. She heard a loud *clang* followed by a *clunk* and then a horrible *screech.*

"You've been ever so kind," said Penelope with a curtsy and then bolted past the confused Clockworker. She could hear the engine slowing as it tried to spit out the wrench. *Please let that buy me some time. Please, please, please,* she thought and ran toward the nearest clock. Each clock was framed in brick, and Penelope figured that the door, if there really *was* a door, would have to be set inside it.

She had almost run the length of one clock when she heard a *whoosh* and felt a soft gust of air. She looked over her shoulder. A long mechanical arm had emerged from high above the rafters. It swooped down, swinging around the room as if looking for prey. She noticed that the two Clockworkers with badges had dragged Dill up onto their platform and were holding him firmly in place. To her horror, the arm came to a halt directly over him.

Penelope froze as she watched the arm descend with a menacing clicking sound. With one swift movement, it plucked Dill up by the coat collar. The arm swung around the room and stopped over an empty spot on the floor. All the

Clockworkers stepped back, their eyes fixed on Dill. The floorboards lifted. A trapdoor opened to a dark hole.

"Dill!" Penelope shouted.

Dill swung his head around to look at her. "*Ruuuun! Don't stop!*" he shouted back before the arm dropped him into the darkness.

Penelope heard the trapdoor slam shut and stifled a scream. Where were they taking him? She had to get him back! But Dill had told her to run. In a burst of panic and speed, Penelope took off. She turned one corner and started down the length of the next clock. Tears filled her eyes, but she kept on running. She had to find the tiny door. A whirring sound overhead made her look up. The arm had swung back around and was moving swiftly in her direction. Penelope realized why no one had bothered to pursue her. It was useless to run. The arm would catch her.

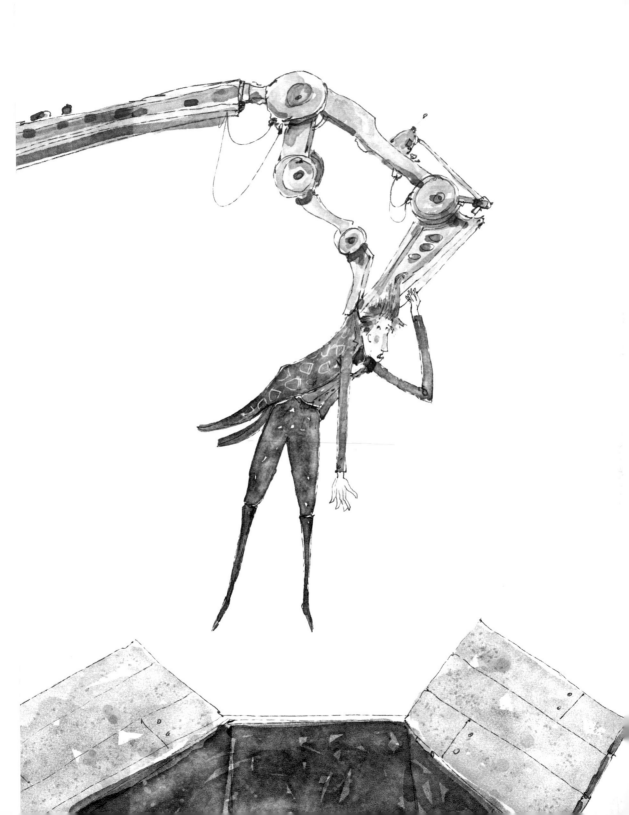

Penelope held on tighter, but every second she held on to disappeared into the next. *Tick-tock-tick-tock.* Up and up Penelope went until her feet dangled uselessly in the air. The second hand was cold and dangerously wet and Penelope could feel her fingers sliding off. The ledge was too narrow to stop her fall. Penelope held on as tightly as she could and reached out with her right foot, desperately straining to lodge it onto the tip of the VII. Thankfully, almost miraculously, her foot caught against the top corner of the sharp metal number.

Before Penelope could feel relief, the second hand moved up another notch and she went with it, leaving the VII below. She craned her neck, looking up. Above her, waiting at the 43 mark, was the minute hand. At that moment, Penelope knew what to do. She would hold on a second *and* on a minute.

Tick-tock-tick-tock. The second hand passed over the minute hand. When the minute hand was at waist level, Penelope raised her legs and wrapped them around its sturdy frame. She locked her ankles and used her position to readjust her grip on the second hand.

Tick. The second hand tried to move forward. Nothing happened. *Tick.* It tried again. Penelope squeezed her eyes shut and, gritting her teeth, pulled down on the second hand as hard as she could. *Tick. Tick. Tick.* She peeled one eyelid open and squinted up. It was working! She was holding on a second. The hand was straining, trying to push its way past 8:43 and 44 seconds.

44 . . . 44 . . . 44 . . .

The second hand struggled to move upward.

44 . . . 44 . . . 44 . . .

Its gears wound tighter and tighter, until . . .

CRACK!

A jagged streak of light danced across the sky and met the spire high above. Blue currents of electricity ran like rivulets down the tower and across the clock face.

The burst of lightning blinded Penelope almost immediately. For a split second, before her eyes were overwhelmed with light, she thought she saw, rising up out of the rain, a glittering white mountain.

Then everything was the flash of lightning and the crack of shattering glass as the great clock exploded and Penelope flew through the air.

-- -- --

If Penelope's world had not turned white, she would have seen the Clockworkers inside the tower stand by helplessly as the clock exploded into the sky. She would have heard a furious ringing fill the air as the mechanical arm swung around and around the vast room, trying to locate the source of all the trouble. Then the great gears that had served the clock so faithfully ground to a halt, sending a chain reaction through the time machine. Springs popped, gears jammed, valves choked, and pistons flew uselessly up and down. Time pieces,

But the figure picked up its pace, growing larger and closer until Penelope gave up. She stood motionless, waiting.

"Hello! Hello!" An excited voice reached Penelope's ears.

"Hello?" Penelope called back.

Moments later a breathless woman was pumping Penelope's arm up and down in greeting. "So glad you've come! So . . . very . . . very glad," she said between little gasps of air.

Penelope stared down into the face of the little old woman, although *little* and *old* hardly described her at all. She *was* little (shorter than Penelope, in fact). And she *was* old (her wrinkles made that obvious). But her tiny figure filled the air with energy and her eyes sparkled with youth. She wore a black-and-white pin-striped shirt with a black ribbon tied in a loose bow around the collar. A jacket with much broader yellow and blue stripes clashed happily against the shirt. It was an altogether invigorating effect.

"Please *do* sit down." The woman swept her arms open as if indicating an entire auditorium of seats for Penelope to choose from.

"Th-thank — you," stammered Penelope. The absence of anything to sit on didn't seem to bother the old woman. She plopped herself down on nothing and gently swayed back and forth as if seated on a rocker.

Penelope gaped at her. "I — I don't see any chairs."

"Pshaw!" answered the woman. "Don't tell me you only believe in what you see! How do you get through life like that?" The woman stopped rocking and leaned forward expectantly, her elbows sitting on nonexistent armrests.

Before Penelope could figure out what to say, the woman popped up and sat down exactly where she had been before. She patted the air next to her invitingly. "Here, dear," she offered. "We'll sit on the couch together. It might be a little easier for you to imagine."

Penelope walked over and slowly lowered herself down, bracing for a fall. Much to her surprise, something firm materialized beneath her and she relaxed into what seemed to be a very comfy couch. Penelope twisted around to see what she was sitting on, but again, she didn't see a thing. When she turned back around, the woman was holding her hands out toward Penelope. One hand was flat, palm up, while the other grasped the air as though it were the handle of a china cup.

"Tea?"

Penelope nodded and tentatively reached out until her fingers met something firm and smooth.

"Careful now, that's a full cup," the woman cautioned. "Sugar?"

Penelope nodded again and watched, dumbfounded, as the woman dropped nothing into the air where Penelope's teacup should be. *Plop. Plop. Plop.*

"Hope you like it sweet," she said. The woman lifted her palm up to her face, tilted her other hand toward her mouth (pinkie finger outstretched), and took a sip of what appeared to be air.

Penelope followed the woman's example and was stunned by the warm, sugary taste that filled her mouth. "It's delicious," she said.

"Mmm . . ." agreed the woman.

Penelope took another sip and then blurted out, "How is this *possible?*"

"It's not," said the woman, leaning forward and placing a nonexistent napkin on Penelope's knee.

"It's not?"

"Of course not! Nothing we do here is possible."

"Then what *is* it?"

"*Im*possible!" answered the woman, clapping her hands together in delight. She must have noticed Penelope's confused expression because she patted her reassuringly on the arm. "The distance between the impossible and the possible is just a hairsbreadth, but few people make the trip. That's why it's so nice to have company. Which reminds me, I haven't introduced myself. How rude!" The woman stretched out her hand. "I'm the Great Moodler."

"*You're* the Great Moodler?!" Penelope was so surprised she dropped her cup of tea. (Luckily the cup wasn't really there, so there wasn't a mess to clean up.)

"You've heard of me?" The Great Moodler's face turned a light shade of pink.

"Yes, I've heard of you! I — I mean *we* — we've been looking for you. Me and my friend Dill."

"And here I am!" replied the Great Moodler with a tinkling little laugh. "Isn't it lovely how that worked out?"

"Yes — I mean, no!" Penelope shook her head fiercely. "It *isn't* working out at all! I need your help. Desperately. Something horrible has happened to Dill. He's trapped in the tower. If he stays there much longer he'll turn into a . . . a Clockworker." She choked back a sob.

"Oh, my!" said the Great Moodler. She placed her arms around Penelope and gave her a gentle squeeze.

"It's not just Dill," continued Penelope. "The *whole* Realm is in danger. I thought I could help, but all my ideas are dried up. And now our friend the

Great Moodler crossed her legs and leaned forward eagerly, eyes fixed on Penelope.

The beginning? It hardly seemed possible to think back that far. "The first thing that happened," said Penelope, trying to collect her thoughts, "was that I landed in the Realm of Possibility."

"Ahhh . . ." said the Great Moodler knowingly.

"I didn't know how I got there or how to get home," continued Penelope. "But then I met Dill, and he told me about you. We went looking for you because he can't find his way and I'm all out of ideas. I want to be a writer, but for some reason I can't moodle anymore. We thought you could help us." By now Penelope's story had started to pick up speed.

"We met the Coo-Coo and he wanted to find you, too. He hoped you could restore the Range of Possibilities. But as soon as we started our search, Chronos's police officers found us idling at an intersection and sent us to prison in the clock tower. That's where we met the Timekeeper. He's the one who told us how to create a no-time. He told me to hang on a second, so I did. I went outside on the ledge of the North Clock and grabbed the second hand. Then there was a storm. A *giant* storm. With lightning . . ."

The Great Moodler nodded her head slowly up and down. "Go on . . ."

Penelope took a jagged breath. "Well, I was hanging on a second when a flash of lightning hit the tower. That's all I remember. Next thing I knew I was here."

The Great Moodler put her cup down on an imaginary table with a firm *chink*. "That's impossible," she said in a hushed and respectful tone.

"It *is*?" asked Penelope, but the Great Moodler didn't seem to be listening.

"*That's* impossible!" she said again, but louder this time. Then she laughed, leaping from the couch and clapping her hands together. She pulled Penelope to her feet and began to dance around, dragging Penelope with her. She

was laughing and shouting at the same time. "That's impossible! That's impossible! Absolutely, fabulously, wonderfully *impossible*!" She stopped to stare intently into Penelope's face. "Do you *know* what you've done?" she asked breathlessly.

"No . . ."

"You broke it."

"The clock?" asked Penelope.

The Great Moodler squeezed Penelope's arms and gave her a tiny shake. "Oh, that was much more than a clock. What you broke, my dear, was a spell. A spell that imprisoned me here and kept the Realm of Possibility under Chronos's control." The Great Moodler flung her hands up in the air. "This is glorious news. Glorious!" She clapped her hands abruptly and began to rub them together. "Come along now! There's not a minute to lose!" The Great Moodler took off running.

"Wait!" Penelope called after her. "What spell did I break?"

"Follow me!" the Great Moodler shouted back.

Penelope ran after her, surprised by how far the little woman had already gone. Once she caught up with her, the Great Moodler began to talk. "When Chronos built the clock tower, he put a spell on it. The clocks of the tower do more than mark time. Much more. They exert a hypnotic power that keeps everyone locked in a horrible malaise."

Penelope wondered what a malaise was. It sounded like a fancy sand-wich spread.

"People are so stuck in the spell, they can't think for themselves. After all, the reason only 217 things are possible is because they *believe* only 217 things are possible. The way to snap people out of their malaise is to show them that *anything* is possible. And the best way to show them that anything is possible is to do something absolutely impossible. Which is *exactly* what you did."

"I did?"

The Great Moodler stopped. She turned to Penelope and fixed her with a deep gaze. "Tell me: If only 217 things are possible, as Chronos would have you believe, what does it mean if something *impossible* happens?"

Penelope thought for a minute. "That 218 things are possible?"

"Well, yes," said the Great Moodler, nodding. "But what if that new possibility is so gloriously impossible it makes people stop and think for a *fraction* of a second: If the impossible is possible, then just how many *possibilities* are possible?" The Great Moodler gripped Penelope's arm, her eyes staring at some unseen horizon. "And in that moment, when this thought dawns on them, they might, just might, snap out of their malaise and believe, even for a minute, in the Realm of Impossibility. If —" Her eyes locked on Penelope. "If they can see it. Now then, we really *must* get busy!"

Off she went again, running through the nothing.

"Where are we going?" Penelope called out, chasing after the Great Moodler's quickly disappearing figure. "I have to get back to Chronos City. I have to find Dill!"

"We're going to find the one thing that can free me and your friend — that can free the entire Realm!" called back the Great Moodler. "The Fancies!"

The Fancies? Images of the drab little creatures floating aimlessly in prison came to Penelope's mind. "I hate to tell you this, but the Fancies are in prison!" she shouted after the Great Moodler.

"Don't be ridiculous!" the Great Moodler shouted back and then immediately took a sharp left. Penelope hurried after her. She felt an incline under her feet and noticed that the bright whiteness all around had faded ever so slightly. The small incline turned into a steep rise. Penelope wasn't gliding anymore. She was trudging. The Great Moodler, however, made rapid progress upward. Penelope wondered what would happen if they got separated. How would she find the Great Moodler if there was nowhere to look?

"Just a little farther!" came a shout from above. Penelope looked up to see the Great Moodler waving at her. "One foot after the other!"

Penelope took a few more steps, her breath coming in short gasps. The white of her surroundings was getting thinner and so was the air. When Penelope finally reached the Great Moodler, the little old woman patted her back. "We're almost there," she said.

Where was there? By now the nothing had completely lost any sort of solidity or color. It was more of a fog, with wisps of shimmering dust that clung to Penelope as she walked. Penelope reached out her hand to move the fog away, but it clung to her fingers.

The Great Moodler took Penelope's elbow and whispered in her ear. "A few more steps . . ." Then, just as Penelope decided they were truly going nowhere, the Great Moodler gave Penelope's elbow a sharp squeeze. "Here we are."

She felt a waft of air touch her face and realized that the Great Moodler was blowing the glittering fog away. When the air cleared, Penelope could see she was standing on what must have been a mountain peak. Above her the sky was blue and full of hope. But below her, nestled right up to the mountain of bright nothingness, closer than she had ever imagined it could be, was something. Something massive, cold, and dark. Something that raised the hair on the back of her neck and brought a pang of fear to her throat.

chapter seventeen

The Shadow was so close Penelope could almost touch it. Almost, but not quite. It was as if an invisible wall separating the two Realms held it back. It swirled around and around, breaking apart and reforming, pressing against the bright nothing with an intensity that could only be described as hunger.

Penelope shivered as a thousand icy spiders ran up her neck. "I thought we were going to see the Fancies," she said through chattering teeth.

"And we are!" trilled the Great Moodler, completely unperturbed by the chilling darkness. "The little darlings should be here any minute. I really can't imagine anything tickling the Fancies more than you breaking Chronos's spell."

Penelope watched the Shadow throw itself against the nothing, pummeling it with unsettling power, then retreating only to rush back again. "Is it safe here?" she asked.

The Great Moodler dismissed the writhing darkness with a wave of her hand. "Of course we're safe! Completely beyond the Shadow of Doubt."

"The Shadow of *Doubt*?" cried Penelope. "Is *that* what that is?"

The Great Moodler looked at Penelope in surprise. "What did you think it was?"

Penelope shrugged. "I — I didn't know."

"Used to be the Realm of Impossibility was visible to everyone. All it took was a little moodling and — *ping!* — there it was. But then Chronos appeared and cast doubt in everyone's mind. Now the Shadow hovers over everything in the Realm of Possibility and nobody knows the impossible is within reach, just beyond the Shadow of Doubt. That's why we've got to get those Fancies."

"But what can the Fancies do?" asked Penelope. As far as she was concerned, the Fancies could hardly stay awake, much less fend off the Shadow.

"Oh-ho," said the Great Moodler, wagging her finger at Penelope. "Never underestimate the power of a Fancy. They can do *anything*. To start with, they can lift the Shadow." The Great Moodler cupped one hand around her right eye and stretched out the other hand as if she were holding a spyglass. She moved the hand in front of her eye back and forth, like she was focusing a lens. "I think I see one now!"

"Where?" Penelope scanned the sky.

"Along the far horizon," said the Great Moodler. "Oh, dear, they're shrunken and half-starved. Just as I expected." She put her arms down and looked at Penelope, nodding toward the Shadow. "See for yourself."

Penelope stared at her.

"Go on then." The Great Moodler nudged Penelope with her elbow. "Give it a try."

Penelope lifted her hands as if she, too, were looking through a spyglass.

She closed her left eye and squinted with her right, until . . . "Oh!" There it was. The Shadow seemed so close it was as if Penelope were standing right in it. A soft, silvery haze directly above the Shadow wavered and then moved. "I think I see something . . ." Penelope said.

"That's it! Keep looking!" urged the Great Moodler.

Penelope kept her eye on the movement. It glimmered like dust caught in a shaft of sunshine. Small black dots swam here and there in the dim light. Suddenly a pair of the black dots blinked. They were eyes!

"I see one! I see one!" Penelope cried. Then she saw another. And another. The haze above the Shadow wasn't a haze at all! It was a swarm of Fancies. They moved like a flock of birds skimming over a dark sea. "There must be thousands of them," said Penelope breathlessly. As she watched, the Fancies came to a halt and then, as if they had choreographed the movement, they dove into the Shadow and vanished. Penelope staggered back. "Wh-what happened to them?"

The Great Moodler took a long look through her telescope. "Thank goodness," she muttered. "They're doing *exactly* what I hoped they would."

Penelope couldn't believe what she was hearing. "You *wanted* them to dive into the Shadow? They'll *die!*"

"They aren't going to die," said the Great Moodler in a soothing voice. "Take a look for yourself."

Looking at the Shadow made Penelope feel like it would suck her in, but she did as she was told. She raised her hands to her face and used her spyglass to search for any sign of the Fancies. Nothing disturbed the Shadow's surface until she saw, out of the corner of her eye, a large chunk of darkness float past and fade into the light of the sun. To her surprise a hole in the Shadow appeared, and streaming out of it were the Fancies! They were pushing and tugging at the Shadow as they flew. Some had it by their toes; others were butting it with their heads.

Penelope turned to look at the Great Moodler. "They're lifting the Shadow!" she said in shock.

The Great Moodler smiled an I-told-you-so smile. "Never underestimate the power of a Fancy," she repeated. "There's *nothing* they can't do. Of course, they'll wear themselves out with all that work, the little sweeties, but we'll just have to fatten them up so they can go back out and finish the job. If we both moodle on whatever tickles our Fancy, we'll have a feast for them in no time."

"Moodle?" Penelope squeaked.

"But of course. It's the best way to feed your Fancy."

"I — I can't," Penelope blurted out.

"Nonsense," said the Great Moodler in the most matter-of-fact voice.

"I'm sorry, but it *isn't* nonsense," insisted Penelope. "I used to be able to moodle all the time. But I *told* you, all my ideas disappeared. They dried up or something . . ." Penelope's voice trailed off.

"My dear," countered the Great Moodler, "anyone who can break Chronos's spell isn't just full of ideas, she's full of possibilities."

Penelope's heart skipped a beat.

Her? Full of possibilities? It couldn't be true.

"You don't understand," Penelope said with a shake of her head. "I tried to use the moodle hat to find you. But I couldn't make the hat work. Nothing came to mind. Dill even called it a . . ." Penelope paused. She didn't want to say the word — the word that had been haunting her ever since she'd heard it. But there was the Great Moodler looking at her, eyebrows raised, waiting for her to finish.

Penelope rushed the words out of her mouth. "He called it an anomaly."

"*Exactly!*" said the Great Moodler with one big, exaggerated nod of her head.

Penelope took a step back. "Exactly? Exactly what?"

"Don't you know what an anomaly is?"

"It's a failure, isn't it?"

"My goodness, no! Quite the opposite. An anomaly is an oddity, a quirk, a rarity. You are all those things and I couldn't be more pleased." The Great Moodler beamed up at Penelope as if she'd won a prize. "You see, an ordinary person would have turned into a Clockworker by now. But you figured out exactly where I was right from the start!"

Penelope's heart skipped. "I did?"

"Didn't you say you moodled on my whereabouts and nothing came to mind?" The Great Moodler held out her arms to embrace the nothing all around. "Ta-da!"

Penelope's jaw dropped. The truth of what the Great Moodler said slowly dawned on her. She remembered the gentle whirring of the hat and the bright, beautiful nothing that opened up inside her as she wore it. No wonder this place looked familiar! She *had* seen it all before! "Do you mean I *did* come up with a big idea?" asked Penelope. "I knew where you were all along?"

"Indeed," said the Great Moodler. "You're a first-rate moodler."

Penelope still couldn't quite believe what she was hearing. "My ideas *aren't* stuck? I *can* be a writer?"

"Of course!" said the Great Moodler. "Now then, let's get busy. We've got work to do. The Fancies will be here any minute."

The Great Moodler whirled around and plopped down into a nonexistent chair. She pulled a DO NOT DISTURB sign out of the nothing and hung it above her head. After settling herself in more comfortably, she let out a deep, humming sigh. As she did, small, brightly colored bubbles streamed out of her ears. Penelope watched as the bubbles danced back and forth, growing larger.

I'm free, thought Penelope. *All along I thought I couldn't moodle. But I could. Miss Maddie was right — all I needed was space. This space.* Penelope felt a surge of excitement. She would help fatten up the Fancies, free Dill, and save the Coo-Coo's home — save the entire Realm! All she had to do was moodle.

At that moment, a few Fancies began to trickle into the Realm of Impossibility. They were pale and wan, shriveled by exertion. Penelope watched as they crowded around the bubbles streaming out of the Great Moodler's head, filling the air with their peeps and squeaks. One of the bubbles started to grow bigger and bigger until . . .

POP!

It broke into a million pieces of light. The Fancies sprang into action, swooping through the air and gobbling up the bright shards. The tiny creatures began to glow as the light danced in their stomachs, puffing them up and up until . . . *PFTTTHHH!* They let out a sound like a balloon losing all its air and spun wildly around. Once they came to a halt, they pounced on another morsel. After each bite, the Fancies were bigger and brighter than before. They filled the sky, bobbing about like gigantic balloons. They were every color of the rainbow and then some. They were so fat, so fluffy, that only the tips of their toes could be seen.

Penelope picked a bit of light off her sleeve and examined it closely. There, glimmering in perfect clarity, were the words:

Fudge is a health food.

"It's a possibility!" said Penelope. Just then a particularly energetic Fancy swooped down and snatched it out of her hand. "Hey!" Penelope tried to snatch

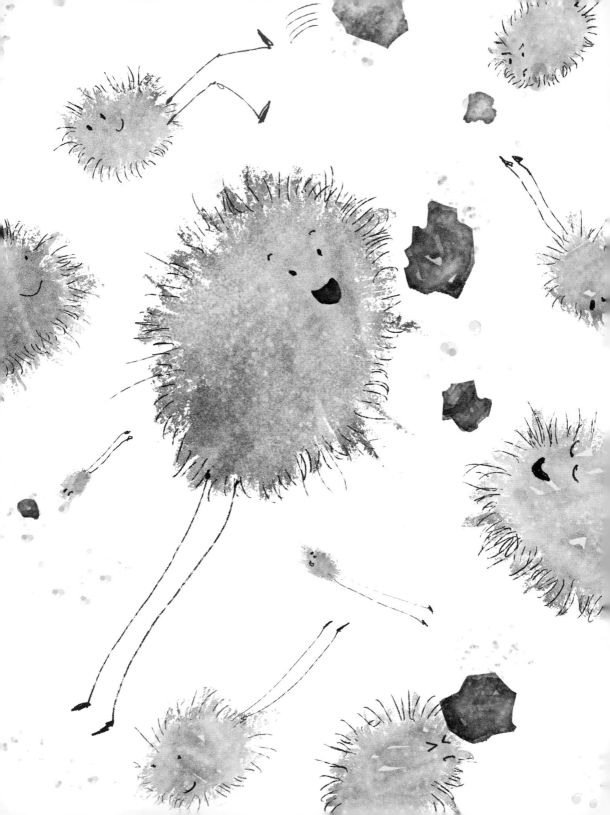

it back, but the Fancy was too fast. It swallowed the possibility and set off to join the others with a loud burp.

Penelope looked at the possibilities falling softly all around her. *I guess there's enough for everybody*, she thought and reached out to catch another one. A flash of light suddenly blinded her and she shielded her eyes before — *plunk* — something soft landed on her chest and tumbled into the front pocket of her overalls. Penelope reached into her pocket and took out a tiny possibility. Squinting, she read the words:

You can do it.

The possibility sent a shock through Penelope and she let out a sharp gasp.

The Great Moodler popped one eye open. "What's all the fuss?"

Penelope cupped her hand around the possibility, hiding it from any hungry Fancies, and walked over to the Great Moodler. "Take a look," she said, opening her hand ever so slightly.

The Great Moodler peered at it and then leaned back with a knowing smile. "You got a good one. That's what I call a Least Possibility. Very tiny, but very powerful. They can grow to be unusually large, if you really consider them. That possibility right there can take you all the way to the moon." She gave Penelope a wink.

Penelope dropped the possibility back into her pocket. By now, more and more Fancies were streaming into the Realm. They

scattered in every direction looking for food. The Great Moodler had returned to her moodling and the air was full of bubbles, some of which had already begun to grow.

Penelope heard a chirping sound and glanced up. An emaciated little Fancy was buzzing around her head. *I'd better get busy*, she thought.

She sat down, crossed her legs, and took out her notebook. She'd been so caught up in trying to escape from the tower, she'd forgotten all about it. Opening it, she stared at a blank page. It was empty, full of nothing, just like the Realm of Impossibility.

She took out her pencil and wrote about all the things that tickled her Fancy. She wrote about drinking tea with the Great Moodler, about following her hunch and discovering the no-time, about the Timekeeper and the Coo-Coo. About everything she'd seen on her journey.

A large group of Fancies crowded around her, vying for spots over her shoulder. They munched hungrily, growing fatter by the moment, feasting on her every word.

On and on she wrote. Here in the Realm of Impossibility, her words took flight above her head, coming to life as the story took shape. And as she wrote, time stood still, waiting patiently for her to finish.

...clockworkers took...

then Dill ate another mushroom

and then we drank tea in the realm

churn uncomfortably. Penelope wrapped her arms around her middle and hugged herself to make the pain go away. "How can that be?" she said, more to herself than to the Great Moodler. "Dill *hates* Chronos. He would never serve him in any way. Never! Not in a million years." Penelope looked up into the Great Moodler's sympathetic eyes. "Something horrible must have happened to him," she insisted. "I can't just leave him there!"

"Nobody said anything about leaving him, dear," said the Great Moodler. "But Dill isn't the only captive. The entire Realm of Possibility is held prisoner by Chronos. Once that clock is restored, the spell will be restored, too. Right now, the clock is still broken and we have a chance to help others believe in the impossible. After the clock starts ticking, our chance is ruined. We *must* help the Fancies."

"But there's no time," pleaded Penelope.

"Oh, but there's all the time in the world," the Great Moodler corrected her.

"*Where?*" Penelope practically screamed.

"Right here," said the Great Moodler, opening her arms as wide as they would go, "in the space of this very moment. Chronos would have you believe you need to save time, but for what? The only time you can spend is the time you have right now. And the time you have right now is all the time in the world." The Great Moodler dropped her hands to her sides. "Time isn't precious, Penelope. You are. As long as you remember that, you're sure to use it wisely." The Great Moodler sat down. "Now then, let's start moodling. I have some Fancies to feed and so do you."

Penelope watched as Fancies floated in. They were exhausted from their efforts and in obvious need of nourishment. She sat down and tried to moodle, but images of Dill in those horrible blue coveralls kept coming to mind. *Is his internal clock broken? Does he even remember me anymore? Does he know what happened to him or is he just a machine?*

Penelope gave her head a quick shake. She had to stay calm. She couldn't afford an outbreak of worry warts. She pressed her lips together and tried to focus. Dill needed her help. She was sure of it. But if she returned to the tower, she risked everything. She might be captured and turned into a Clockworker. If it could happen to Dill, it could happen to her! But the Great Moodler said staying here and feeding the Fancies was crucial. Besides, it was safe here. Even if they didn't succeed in lifting the Shadow and the Realm of Possibility was lost in doubt again, Penelope was back to her old moodling self. It felt so amazing she didn't want to stop — if only she had a little more time!

Penelope looked over at the Great Moodler. She was stretched out with her feet up as if she were sitting on a recliner. Her eyes were closed and bubbles streamed out of her head. The Great Moodler had said Penelope would *never* have more time. That people were what really mattered.

Penelope got to her feet. *I can't save time*, she thought. *But I can save Dill.*

She walked right up to the edge of the shimmering mountain and stared out over the Shadow. She remembered Dill telling her that people used to ride the Fancies. All she had to do was capture one and then ride it to the tower. If she moved quickly, maybe she could rescue Dill and be back before the Great Moodler even noticed. That is, if she didn't get caught. Penelope shuddered. She couldn't think about that right now.

A dull blue Fancy about the size of a cantaloupe emerged out of the darkness, and Penelope waved it over. *I'd better fatten you up*, she thought, and took out her notebook. She had already used up all the paper, so she turned to the inside back cover. She only had time for one amazing moodle. Penelope stared at the nothing all around her. For a brief moment she saw it reflected in her own mind. She sat, basking in the nothing until — *pop!* — an idea inspired by Dill came to mind. She started to write:

Mushrooms are a delectable fungus.

Some are small; others humongous.

They grow on the ground.

Can be found all around.

We'll never starve with them among us.

As Penelope wrote, the Fancy gobbled up every word. When she was done, the creature chittered in pleasure and did a series of quick somersaults. After each somersault, it landed in front of Penelope, twice the size it had been before. When it was through bouncing around, it was almost as big as a pony.

Perfect! thought Penelope and glanced quickly over her shoulder at the Great Moodler. The little old lady was still busy moodling. *Well, here goes . . .* Penelope approached the Fancy and, with a little leap, tried to mount it. She grabbed ahold of where she imagined the neck might be, but all she managed to do was knock the Fancy off the mountain ledge. It let out a surprised screech, but then fluttered back to where Penelope stood.

"Sorry," whispered Penelope. She backed away to regroup. *How can I climb on top of a puff of air? It's impossible.* Penelope suppressed a giggle. Of course it was impossible! Everything in this Realm was impossible.

She turned back to the Fancy and imagined a tiny trampoline near her feet. She took two quick steps and a short hop. Sure enough, she landed on a firm but springy surface and shot into the air. She reached for the Fancy and, in her mind, its fluff turned to fur. When she grasped the creature, Penelope felt something soft and thick under her fingers. She held on tight, swinging her legs up and over before landing firmly on the Fancy's back.

To her delight the Fancy lifted into the air and zoomed away, heading

straight for the Realm of Possibility. When they crossed over the Shadow, Penelope felt a chill grab hold of her toes and move up her legs. She glanced down and saw the darkness churning like a rough sea below. Doubt gripped her mind. *I'm riding on nothing but air! I'm going to drop like a rock!*

And so that is *exactly* what she did.

chapter nineteen

The Fancy let out a hideous scream, its little feet paddling helplessly against the rush of air. Penelope tried to scream, too, but her throat clamped shut. Her stomach flattened against her ribs, and she clutched the Fancy, but there was nothing there to hold. The fur just melted in her fingers. She gulped for air, and as her lungs filled, she found her voice again.

"*STOP!*"

But the Fancy didn't stop. If anything it fell faster, straight through the Shadow. The force of the wind pushed Penelope's cheeks up against her eyes and lifted her mouth into a gruesome grin. Her thoughts ran in every direction, like marbles dumped on the floor. She didn't even try to gather them up as complete panic set in. She began to shiver uncontrollably and her teeth would have chattered if she wasn't clenching them so tightly.

Whoosh! They fell through the Shadow and into the dull sky of the Realm. Penelope looked down and saw the world rushing up to meet her. The Fancy gained speed as it fell, and the wind shifted to a high-pitched whistle. Penelope wanted to cover her ears but was afraid she might fall off. As soon as this thought occurred to her, her knees loosened what little grip they had and she slid forward until . . .

THWACK!

horrible enchantment,
to her so they could e[...]

But Dill kept wa[...]
didn't even look back.
It was as if their brain[...]
switched off. The Cloc[...]
continued their stiff m[...]
door and Dill went wi[...]

Penelope stood t[...]
Dill really left her?

She turned back[...]
debris. She was so cau[...]
arm snaking through t[...]
fingers opened with an[...]
looked up, but it was t[...]
around the strap of her[...]
swift tug she was lifted[...]
and dropped into the
waiting trapdoor.

The Fancy fell through a flock of birds, hitting one and sending it spiraling off course. The rest of the birds screeched in dismay and scattered in every direction. One bird flew backward into Penelope's face. Penelope forgot all about falling off the Fancy as she spit out a mouthful of feathers. The feathers reminded her of the Coo-Coo and for a brief moment the delightful memory of flying with the giant bird flashed through her mind. She grabbed the memory and held it tightly, imagining the peaceful exhilaration she felt on the Coo-Coo's back. At that moment, something completely unexpected happened. The Fancy began to slow and the horrible sinking feeling abated. The Fancy was doing exactly what she imagined!

Penelope quickly pictured the Fancy flying along at a gentle pace, with the world passing below like a lazy river. Next she envisioned the force of the wind reduced to a summer breeze. To her great relief, both of these things happened.

Penelope relaxed and dared to take a peek at the ground. It was no longer a blurry mass zooming toward her. Instead, she could clearly make out the contours of the City. The roads were long and narrow, crossing one another at sharp angles, with buildings on either side. Traffic lights dotted the way and cars moved slowly up and back, stopping at regular intervals. One of the roads was three times as wide as the others, heading straight toward the tower.

to strangle the poor †

responded to it imm

up at the door leadin

the end of the line, s

takable figure of Dil

Dang-dung. Dan

In one single n

Penelope pull

little door in the bri

open, one of its hing

Penelope caref

the door. The Fanc

can't come in here.

made a sad little chi

was just too small.

"Wait for me .

By now the line of

in unison down the

reached the door ar

"Diiiillll

or if she set off the

-- -- --

Penelope tried to sit up but lay back down immediately. Her head felt like it was floating on a string while her stomach danced a jig. *Where am I?* she wondered.

Tall stone walls dripping with moisture surrounded her on every side. A dim light filtered down from an opening high above. She had no memory of falling — no memory other than the swift jerk of the arm and the sickening feeling of being dropped. After that her mind was blank. Penelope closed her eyes, willing her memory back into place.

"Welcome," said a cool, dry voice.

Penelope's eyes popped open. A face was looking down at her from above. It belonged to a man with a sharp nose and an even sharper chin. His mouth was unusually small, with lips so thin they were hardly distinguishable. He reminded Penelope of a snake.

Penelope scrambled to her feet, bracing herself against the cool wall. "Who are you? Let me out of here!"

"I don't think so," said the man with a smug little smile. "Now that I have you, I think I'll keep you. After all, I've had so much fun getting to know your *friend* Dill." He said the word *friend* as if it were a distasteful thing.

Penelope swallowed hard. "What have you done to him?"

"What have *I* done?" The man leaned over the pit and pointed a long finger at her. "What have *you* done is the question. Did you know that you stopped every clock in the Realm when you destroyed the north clock? Every single clock came to a complete standstill. Can you imagine all that wasted time? All those perfectly good seconds, minutes, and hours gone. Naturally somebody had to make up for it all, and Dill, well, he practically *volunteered*."

Penelope glared up at the man. "Dill would never volunteer to be a Clockworker. Never!"

The man just smiled. "I want you to know that Dill makes an excellent

Clockworker. As will you . . ." He reached into his pocket and took out a gold watch, which he dangled in the air.

Penelope shrank back against the wall, her heart pounding. She suddenly realized who she was talking to. This man wasn't some Clockworker she could outmaneuver or a Wild Bore she could outwit. This was Chronos himself! If he could cast a spell over the entire Realm and banish the Great Moodler, what would he do to *her*?

Chronos began to lower the watch down into the pit. "Did I say you destroyed *all* the clocks? What I meant to say was all but one. This little watch is actually what keeps the Clockworkers in my power and the Realm running on time. Soon I will use it to reset the north clock and then time will be on *my* side again. But first there's something I need to do."

By now the watch was hanging above Penelope's head, too high to reach, but close enough that she could hear its hands moving rhythmically — *tick-tock-tick-tock* — around its white face.

"Can you tell me what time it is?" asked Chronos.

The words pulled at Penelope with a strange power and she couldn't help but look up. When she did, the watch caught her eye and wouldn't let go. She tried to look away, but her eyes were locked on the endless motion of the second hand. Before she knew it, her arms and legs were frozen as well.

Tick-tock-tick-tock. The incessant ticking grew strangely louder.

Don't listen to it! she told herself. She tried humming a song in her head, reciting important dates, and telling herself familiar stories, but it was impossible to shut out the sound. The ticking seeped in, drowning her in its monotony.

"Penelope . . ." Chronos said in a soft, low voice. "What time is it?"

But Penelope couldn't hear his words — she couldn't even hear her own thoughts. All she could hear was the watch.

TICK-TOCK-TICK-TOCK.

Its sound ricocheted against the walls of the pit until . . .

BBBBBRINGGGG!

A loud alarm shook the air. Chronos let out a shout of delight before quickly retracting the watch. "So sorry, but we'll have to save our fun for later. Time has come and I'm needed elsewhere." He pulled the watch up the rest of the way and snapped it closed.

When he did, Penelope staggered forward, as if released from a spell. She stood there, struggling to make sense of what had just happened.

"I hate to leave a job unfinished," continued Chronos, "but I must go synchronize the clocks in the tower. Until I get back, I suggest you start getting used to the idea of becoming a Clockworker. After all," he added with a nasty little chuckle, "there's not the *least* possibility of escape."

Chronos's words struck Penelope like a blow. A Clockworker? Is that what Chronos used the pocket watch for? To turn people into his slaves?

Penelope looked around wildly. She had to get out of there! She ran her fingers over the wall, searching for a handhold, but the stones were all too smooth and damp. In desperation, she tried digging around the flagstones of the floor, but all she managed to do was bruise her hands.

There has to be a way out of here. Think, Penelope! Think! But no matter how hard she tried, Penelope *couldn't* think. Her head felt clouded and dull. When she searched for the clear, bright nothing — the place inside herself where ideas came from — she found a dense fog hovering in her mind.

Penelope slumped to the ground and rested her head on her knees. *I'll never rescue Dill. Why did I come here? The Great Moodler is probably wondering where I am. Now I'll turn into a Clockworker and be stuck here forever. Chronos is right. There's not the least possibility of escape!*

A cry welled up from deep inside her, bursting from her lips. But instead of a sob ricocheting against the walls, a small speck of darkness flew from her lips and landed at her feet. Penelope jumped up and stared down at the black speck. As she watched, it quickly grew from a speck into a spot and then a puddle. The puddle stretched into a thick ribbon of black. Long wavering appendages sprouted from its sides — four in total. These appendages sprouted appendages of their own. One, two, three, four, five each. They were hands with fingers. And feet with toes. And then, as if on cue, a head grew at the top.

Penelope couldn't look away from the dark shape on the ground. It looked like her shadow, but it was deeper and darker than any shadow she'd ever seen. It moved and swayed of its own accord, free from the mastery of a sun that had not cast it. Its arms drifted open and its fingers waved, beckoning Penelope down.

Penelope backed away into what little corner there was. *This is not happening. This is not happening. This is not happening*, she told herself.

But it was.

The darkness spread soundlessly toward her. Penelope stood shivering, breathing in short, sharp gasps, as the moisture in the air turned to frost. The puddle crept across the stone floor, inching closer and closer until it lapped at Penelope's toes.

Penelope lifted one foot and then the other, but the puddle just grew wider until it seeped under her feet. Her shoes were the first thing to disappear. Her ankles were next. Penelope was frozen, as the darkness gathered around her, sliding up her body, disappearing her bit by bit. There went her knees and thighs, then her torso and arms until, finally, it swallowed her head.

chapter twenty

If Penelope could have fallen she would have, but there was no telling which direction was up and which was down. It was as if she were floating in a dark vacuum. A bitter cold pressed against her like a blanket of ice — dry, heavy ice. She was afraid to breathe. Afraid the cold would grip her lungs and stop her heart.

Penelope held her breath as long as she could, until finally it was too much. She gasped, and when she did, the dark slid down her throat.

That's when the whispering began, speaking with soundless words. *There's not the least possibility of escape. There's not the least possibility of escape.* The words ran over and over through her mind until they found a way out of her mouth.

"There's not the least possibility of escape," she muttered. "There's not the least possibility of escape." Silence quickly swallowed the words, but not before Penelope realized that saying them had given her an odd sort of comfort. Why?

There's not the least possibility of escape. This time she kept the words to herself, looking at them in her mind with a detached curiosity: The darkness had come. It had taken her for its own. There wasn't the least possibility of escape.

And then it struck her. The Least Possibility. Of course! How could she have forgotten? There *was* the Least Possibility. It was in her pocket.

Penelope reached inside her pocket with frozen fingers, fumbling until . . .

there! She felt it. A slight warmth. Penelope carefully brought out the tiny possibility and cradled it in her palm. It was so dull and faded, she could hardly make out the words: *You can do it.*

The darkness immediately began to move. It circled Penelope, slowly at first and then faster and faster until it was a whirling, sucking gloom. Penelope clutched the Least Possibility to her chest. Its warmth spread from her hand and into her heart. She opened her fingers and looked down at the tiny speck. It was glowing again, faint but true.

You can do it.

By now the dark was a feverish tempest, whipping around her with desperate force. Penelope didn't worry that it would knock her to the ground or fling her into the air. There was nowhere to go — the darkness was all there was.

Except . . . except for the light she held in her hand. Did she dare lose it?

Fighting the pressure of the storm, Penelope raised her hand, palm flat, above her head. The Possibility grew heavier and its light shone brighter, but the dark whirled only faster.

You can do it, she told herself.

She braced the Least Possibility with both hands, but even that wasn't enough.

You can do it.

Penelope gritted her teeth as her arms began to shake from the weight.

In a fury of movement, the dark snatched the Least Possibility from her hand and flung it upward and away. But instead of disappearing, it hovered above the dark chaos like a star, piercing it in a hundred places. Penelope looked up and saw something that surprised her — bricks. She had thought the darkness was trying to take her away, but it wasn't. The sucking, pulling, and whirling was just the black disappearing like water down a drain.

More and more of the pit came into view as the dark slipped away. Now Penelope could see her shoulders. Then her waist, her legs, and her feet! Down, down, down went the darkness until it was a puddle on the floor once again. Penelope watched it shrink until it was the teeny tiniest bit of matter and then — *pop!* — it disappeared altogether.

The Least Possibility crashed to the floor, shattering against the stones into a million tiny sparks. The sparks rushed to one another like magnets and soon they formed a small cluster.

Penelope remembered the Great Moodler's words about Least Possibilities. *They can grow to be unusually large, if you really consider them. That possibility right there can take you all the way to the moon.* Penelope didn't need to go all the way to the moon. She just needed to get to the top of the pit.

"I can do it!" Penelope shouted, and the words poured over her like sunshine.

The cluster of light turned into a mound.

"I can do it!"

The mound turned into a hill. Penelope scrambled up it. *I can do it . . . I can do it . . .* The hill was growing so fast that no matter how hard she ran, the top was beyond reach. She could feel the wind in her face as the walls of the pit rushed past. Still the hill grew higher and wider until the pit itself began to crumble. In a matter of seconds, the Least Possibility burst out into the open, sending stones flying. Penelope slid down the side of the hill, landing with a small hop on the ground. And with that, she was free.

-- -- --

Penelope found herself in a room that was hardly more than a cave. A few lights hung from a low ceiling and a set of worn stairs cut through the rough stone walls. She had no idea when Chronos would return, but she didn't want to be here when he did. Now there was only one thing left to do — find Dill and get back to the Great Moodler!

Penelope sprinted up the stairs for several stories until they stopped at a gray metal door. She caught her breath, then opened it a crack and stuck her head out. She recognized the dark terminal where Officer X had taken her and Dill when they first arrived at the tower. She remembered it as a busy place, filled with Clockworkers and cars. This time, other than a few fluorescent bulbs flickering on and off, it was completely empty.

Penelope saw a driveway off to her left and headed straight for it. She ran up its steep incline, her shoes smacking the concrete floor and her breath coming loud and hard. When she reached the top, the driveway emptied out into the vast courtyard between the tower and the Timely Manor. Above her a blue sky — not gray, but *real* blue — peeked out from behind fading clumps of darkness.

The Fancies are lifting the Shadow! she thought with a thrill of joy. *They're doing it! They're really doing it!*

If the Fancies were still able to lift the Shadow, that meant one thing — Chronos hadn't restored his spell. There was still time to save Dill, *if* she could find him. *You can do it*, she told herself. *You can —*

THWAP!

Penelope staggered backward as a mass of blue fur engulfed her. She laughed and hugged the Fancy. "I'm glad to see you, too," she said and climbed onboard. "Now let's go find Dill and get out of here."

The Fancy took off, heading up the sides of the tower. As they flew, Penelope scanned the ground, but there were no Clockworkers, or cars, or even guards patrolling the parapet around the Manor. "Where is everyone?" she whispered.

In answer, the Fancy sped up. It reached the far corner of the clock tower and rounded it smartly before coming to a halt. Below them, covering every inch of the courtyard's northern quadrant in tight, neat rows, were the Clockworkers.

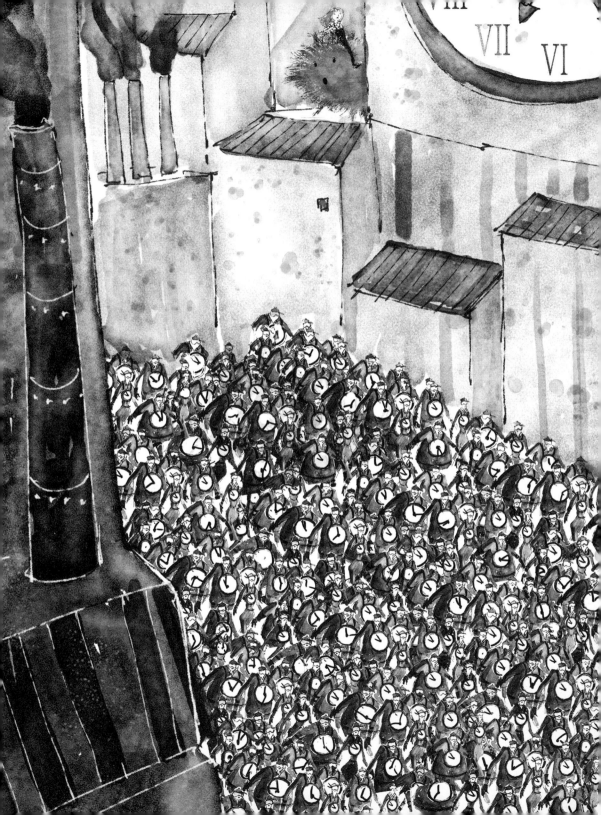

All of the Clockworkers. Thousands and thousands of them stood facing the Timely Manor, arms at their sides. They looked straight ahead, staring at a set of double doors at the top of a grand staircase. There was a hush in the air, as if they were waiting for something.

Penelope searched the crowd for Dill. He must be there, but which one was he? They were all dressed the same, with blue hats that obscured their faces. Her only hope was to see a hint of his red hair.

At that moment the doors of the Timely Manor opened and Chronos stepped out. Penelope crouched down on the Fancy's back, urging it to fly even higher. The Fancy hugged the side of the tower as it flew, and its blue fur turned gray, blending in with the stone wall and forming a perfect camouflage.

As Penelope watched, Chronos approached a microphone at the top of the ornate staircase and spoke. "You have been off the clock too long. Trouble has sprung from your idleness." He pointed at the sky and the fading Shadow, his thin lips pressed into a frown. "Soon I will restore order to the Realm. The clocks will begin again and so will your work!" He dug into his pocket and brought out his watch. Gripping it in his fist, he held it up in the air. "Never forget," he shouted, "time is on *my* side!"

Penelope stared down at Chronos. The blue sky and sunshine highlighted his pale, pinched face. She remembered looking up at him from the pit. He had looked powerful then, but from here he looked small and . . . and something else. Unhappy? Was that what she saw in his face? *No*, decided Penelope, *he doesn't look unhappy. He looks . . . he looks . . . afraid.*

The thought rang out in Penelope's mind with absolute clarity, and she knew she had hit upon the truth. Chronos was afraid. Afraid the Shadow of Doubt would fade. Afraid the Clockworkers would see beyond it. Afraid the people of the Realm would believe in the impossible and the Great Moodler would return.

Penelope thought about the Realm of Impossibility. Even though she couldn't see it or touch it, it was somehow *there*. And in its there-ness was a great power. According to the Great Moodler, the two Realms — the Realm of Possibility and Impossibility — were intermingled. One couldn't exist without the other. Chronos hid that fact behind the Shadow, but the Shadow was fading and, as it faded, his power went with it.

"Time is on *my* side!" Chronos screamed again. His voice had a whining undertone that Penelope hadn't noticed before. She imagined him stomping his foot like a three-year-old and tried not to laugh.

Chronos opened his fist and the pocket watch swung back and forth on its chain. He held the swaying watch up in front of the microphone and a soft ticking sound filled the air. *Tick-tock-tick-tock-tick-tock*. But just as it had done when Penelope was in the pit, the ticking didn't stay soft for long. It grew louder and more insistent until Chronos didn't need the microphone at all.

The Clockworkers stared straight ahead, eyes trained on the watch. "Tick-tock-tick-tock-tick-tock," they chanted in unison. With each word, a wisp of something like smoke escaped their lips. Soon a dark haze hovered above each Clockworker. Each haze grew thicker as they chanted until it began to take on a shape — a ghostly, human shape.

The shapes sprouted long waving arms and beckoning fingers that sent chills down Penelope's back. She had seen this darkness before — it had plagued her in the pit. Darker than the dark of night, the forms were like small black holes in the sky. Penelope knew they wouldn't stay small for long. Sure enough, as soon as a dark form fully materialized, it lifted up into the air, stretching its long fingers toward the faint Shadow waiting above. With a sickening feeling, Penelope realized what she was seeing. Doubts.

So *that's* what had popped out of her mouth in the pit! She had unleashed her doubts and now the Clockworkers were doing the same.

"Tick-tock-tick-tock-tick-tock," they chanted. There was a horrible sucking sound and a bitter wind raced across the courtyard. The poor Fancy, high up in the air, rocked back and forth from its force.

Whatever fear there was left in Penelope melted into rage. "Go!" she shouted to her Fancy. The Fancy flew straight toward the Timely Manor, the wind whistling through its fur. Penelope tried to imagine it flying faster than a rocket — faster than the speed of light. *Whoosh!* She landed at the top of the stairs, jumped off the Fancy, and bolted toward the doors. Above them she saw a stone carving of a clock with rolling ocean waves on either side. The waves crested and then crashed, wrapping long tendrils of foam around an hourglass filled with sand. Below the clock, carved in elaborate scrolling letters, were the words:

TIME AND TIDE WAIT FOR NO ONE.

Penelope wrenched the Manor's doors open and rushed inside. She was met by a long empty corridor lit from the floor. A row of dim lights outlined a path through the gloom and cast a weak glow on the walls, which were lined with grandfather clocks. The clocks were stooped with age, their shoulders hunched as if bearing the weight of time. Each clock had a dull silver pendulum hanging like a beard from its flat gray face. Something about the clocks made them look human.

Penelope ran down the corridor as fast as she could. At first, the corridor followed the curve of the building, but before long it twisted around in a maze of tight spirals. Penelope ran for what seemed like miles, but the corridor never ended. In fact, it never even seemed to change. Every clock she passed looked exactly like the next. Time slipped away (did it even exist?) and still she ran.

"*Please* stop it," Penelope begged.

Chronos watched her calmly.

"*Please* . . ."

Chronos's hand hovered over the key. "I suppose I could let him go if you would do *one* thing for me."

"Yes!" cried Penelope, frantic. "Whatever you want."

Chronos removed the key and the clock stood still. He took out his pocket watch. "I don't know how you escaped the pit, but you won't get away from me this time." He raised the watch in the air and let it sway back and forth. "Let's pick up where we left off, shall we? Tell me what time it is, Penelope." His voice was soft and beckoning.

The watch tugged at Penelope, but she looked away.

"*Tell me what time it is*," repeated Chronos. Now there was an unpleasant edge to the words.

"Just a moment," Penelope pleaded. She knew that if she looked at the watch and listened to its ticking, she would become a Clockworker. If she didn't, Dill would be pressed for time. The situation was impossible!

Nothing is impossible, she told herself. She'd seen that with her own eyes. *If nothing is impossible, then there must be a way out. But what is it?*

"Penelope . . ." Chronos's voice was downright threatening.

"Five minutes," said Penelope. "Just give me five minutes."

Chronos's eyes narrowed and he smiled a tight little smile. "I'll give you thirty seconds." He nodded curtly at the pocket watch. "The clock is ticking."

Penelope sat down on the floor and closed her eyes. She rested her head in her hands and placed her fingers over her ears, blocking out the sound of the watch. *What time is it?*

The watch would tell her a number. But what did that number really mean? To the Timekeeper, time was categorized by type — good time, bad time, borrowed time, and due time. To the Coo-Coo, time was the song of life. To Dill, time was what made mushrooms grow. But what was time to *her*?

Penelope's thoughts drifted this way and that until they ran their course and disappeared. At that moment, a soft sound, like a tiny silver bell, rang inside her head. Penelope forgot everything and listened. The sound danced and leapt, and everywhere it touched thoughts fell away until there was, for the briefest moment, a warm, white nothing.

At that moment, Penelope heard the voice of the Great Moodler: *The only time you can spend is the time you have right now. And the time you have right now is all the time in the world. Time isn't precious, Penelope. You are. As long as you remember that, you're sure to use it wisely.*

"Stop that this instant!" screamed Chronos. "You will *not* moodle under my watch!"

Penelope opened her eyes. She looked up at the watch swaying back and forth and a word popped out of her mouth. She didn't remember thinking the word. It was just there, waiting to be said.

"Now."

A look of horror crossed Chronos's face. "*What* did you say?"

Penelope got to her feet. "I said, the time is Now."

The pocket watch stopped swaying and its hands began to spin at a maddening speed. Chronos snatched the watch back and tapped furiously at its glass face. "What have you done?" he screamed at Penelope. He tried to wind the watch, moving the crown back and forth in a desperate attempt to stop the runaway hands. But they only went faster until there was a loud *crack!* — and the pocket watch shattered. Tiny wheels, screws, and bits of glass spilled everywhere. Chronos fell to his knees. "Nooooo . . ." His hands swept the floor, trying desperately to salvage the broken bits of his masterpiece.

chapter twenty-two

Penelope stared up into the biggest, bluest sky she'd ever seen. The Shadow of Doubt was gone and the garish green lights of the tower destroyed. Sunshine poured out over everything, bringing the world alive with color. Even the gray concrete of the Manor was radiant in the light of day.

Penelope felt a slight shudder under her feet and she glanced over at Dill. "Did you feel that?"

He nodded. "Let's get out of here." Before they could move, they heard a loud groan and a fine cloud of dust suddenly filled the air, followed by a rush of falling rocks.

"*Run!*" shouted Dill.

They sprinted across the veranda and took the stairs two at a time (three at a time, in Dill's case), not stopping to look back until they reached the ground. The carved clock above the Manor door was gone. Instead of TIME AND TIDE WAIT FOR NO ONE, the quote now read: . . . ME AND . . . I . . . WAIT FOR . . . ONE.

"That was close," said Penelope.

"Too close," agreed Dill. "We'd better keep moving."

They set off toward the far side of the courtyard where a set of gates led out into the City. Crossing the courtyard, however, was no easy matter. The earthquake had destroyed much of the Timely Manor and chunks of concrete littered the ground. The wreckage would have been easy to navigate if not for the Clockworkers. They were a mass of confusion. Without the ticking of the clock tower to guide them, their steps had lost all rhythm. They turned this way and that like broken windup toys. They tripped over the rubble and one another, bumping into Dill and Penelope in the process.

"You-must-ex-cuse-me. I-do-beg-your-par-don," they repeated over and over again to no one in particular.

"What's wrong with them?" asked Penelope.

"They're lost," explained Dill. "There aren't any clocks to dictate their movements."

"Well, they certainly haven't lost their manners. Why aren't they trying to stop our escape?"

"Oh, Clockworkers aren't so bad," Dill admitted, neatly sidestepping one who was just about to back into him. "Their worst habit is doing what they're told. Without someone to boss them around, they're harmless."

Penelope looked over at Dill. Although he had lost the hat, he was still wearing the blue coveralls of a Clockworker. "For a while, I thought . . . I thought you were one of them."

got to the part about the Great Moodler, he grabbed her arm. "So you found her?"

"You won't believe it, but I had an idea where she was all along!" Penelope told him the whole story of the the no-time and meeting the Great Moodler in the Realm of Impossibility.

Dill hung on every word. When he heard about the Fancies lifting the Shadow of Doubt, he looked back at the Fancy. "That's amazing. Outstanding. Truly impressive." The Fancy turned bright pink and then gold with pride.

"There's nothing a Fancy can't do," said Penelope, quoting the Great Moodler. "All they needed was a little fattening up."

By now they had reached the far side of the tower and the gates to Chronos City loomed in front of them. Pushing against the gates, in a useless attempt to open them, was the Timekeeper. When he saw Dill and Penelope, a huge smile spread across his face. "Hello! Hello!" he cried, waving them over. "You'll never believe what happened. I was having a short nap when the clocks in the tower went crazy. They all went off at once. It was a horrible racket. The earth began to shake and the tower along with it. I thought the tower would collapse, but then the clocks grew silent and I suddenly knew what time it was."

shouldn't be a problem. We'll moodle up a Least Possibility. And with thousands of people here in the City to consider it, we'll eventually restore the Range." The Great Moodler turned to Penelope. "Are you willing to give it a try?"

"Oh, yes!"

The Great Moodler turned to Dill. "And you?"

Dill stood up tall. "I'll do what I can even though I don't have my moodle hat."

"*Coo-coo . . . coo-coo,*" sang the bird ever so softly. "Would this help . . . *you-you?*" He slipped his head under his wing and pulled it out again. There, between his beak, was a shiny flat object.

"My moodle hat!" Dill rushed forward and the Coo-Coo dropped it into his outstretched hands. "Wherever did you find it?"

"It caught my eye as I . . . *flew-flew* . . . over the wasteland. I thought someone . . . *threw-threw* . . . it away."

"Someone *did*," said Dill. "It was the awful Officer X. I thought I'd never see it again." He clutched the hat to his chest. "Thank you," he said to the bird, his eyes shining.

Just then, they heard a commotion and a figure emerged from the gates of the Timely Manor. His clothes were dusty and torn, and he walked as if in a dream, but Penelope recognized him right away. "It's *Chronos*," she said in alarm.

Everyone watched as Chronos caught sight of a Clockworker. He grabbed
her arm and gesticulated wildly at the tower. The Clockworker didn't seem the
least bit interested and instead held out a possibility for him to consider. Chronos
shoved the possibility aside and ran to the next Clockworker and the next, but

Penelope waved and waved until

her friends turned into tiny dots

and then disappeared.

acknowledgments

All my thanks to the original Great Moodler — Brenda Ueland — who gave me "the impulse to write one small story." I hope you are pleased.

Profound gratitude to: my editor, Tracy Mack, whose wisdom and kindness brought this book into being; my agent, Marietta Zacker, for making my anything possible — you're a wonder; to Emellia Zamani for recognizing Penelope early on and to Kait Feldmann for her finishing touches; to all the remarkably talented people at Scholastic, especially Marijka Kostiw for her brilliant design and Monique Vescia for her careful copyedits; and to Lee White for bringing it all alive with his illustrations.

I owe a debt to Norton Juster for capturing my imagination so thoroughly with *The Phantom Tollbooth*.

I am grateful to the Writer's Colony at Dairy Hollow for the extraordinary gift of uninterrupted time.

Many thanks to Meredith Davis, Sherrie Peterson, and Cindy Shortt for reading this manuscript when it was lumpy. Your feedback and encouragement helped give it real shape.

To Robyn Cloughley, thank you for holding a supportive space so wide, for so many years.

Deep appreciation to Anne Marie Chenu for teaching me you can't fall off the path; and to Peg Syverson for all her mindful, active care.

Love and endless gratitude to my parents, Darwin and Carolyn Britt, who gave me all the time in the world; and to my family, for always being there.

Special thanks to Jerri Romine, who knew — beyond a shadow of doubt — that this story had to be told. I couldn't have written it without you.

Finally, and forever, thank you to my husband, Justin Pehoski. Your grace and goodness give me courage.

about the author

Paige Britt grew up in a small town, with her nose in a book and her head in the clouds. She studied journalism in college and theology in graduate school but never stopped reading children's books for life's most important lessons. In addition to writing, she loves to sit and moodle. (If you don't know what moodling is, you should probably read this book.) Paige lives in Georgetown, Texas, with her husband. *The Lost Track of Time* is her first novel.

about the illustrator

Lee White is an artist and teacher who loves watercolor, printmaking, and climbing trees. He spends his days splashing paint in his backyard studio, where there are absolutely no clocks allowed! He has illustrated more than fifteen books and shown in galleries across the country, from Los Angeles to New York. He lives in Portland, Oregon, with his wife and their young son.

The
jacket art and interior
illustrations for this book were
created in watercolor and digital mixed
media by Lee White. The text of this book was set
in 12 point Perpetua, which was designed for Monotype
Imaging by English sculptor and typeface designer Eric Gill.
Gill is known most famously for his self-named face, Gill Sans,
a font that made him a legacy to typography and has stood the test
of time. Gill began work on Perpetua in 1925, but the finished
design wasn't released until 1929, when it appeared in a transla-
tion of Walter H. Shewring's *The Passion of Perpetua and Felicity*,
from which the font took its name. Perpetua was selected for
this book both for its classic beauty and its resonance with
the book's theme of time. The display type was set in Love
Letter Typewriter, a modern typeface designed in 1996
by Dixie's Delights. This book was printed and bound
by Tien Wah in Singapore, and manufacturing
was supervised by Francine O'Bum. The
book was designed by Marijka
Kostiw.